Swallowing Stones

Also by Joyce McDonald

Devil on My Heels

Shades of Simon Gray

Shadow People

Comfort Creek

Mail-Order Kid

Homebody

Swallowing Stones

JOYCE MCDONALD

EMBER

Text copyright © 1997 by Joyce McDonald
Cover photograph copyright © 2012 by Shutterstock

All rights reserved. Published in the United States by Ember, an imprint of Random House Children's Books, a division of Random House, Inc., New York. Originally published in hardcover in the United States by Delacorte Press, an imprint of Random House Children's Books, New York, in 1997.

Ember and the E colophon are registered trademarks of Random House, Inc.

Visit us on the Web! randomhouse.com/teens

Educators and librarians, for a variety of teaching tools,
visit us at randomhouse.com/teachers

The Library of Congress has cataloged the hardcover edition of this work as follows:
McDonald, Joyce.
Swallowing stones / Joyce McDonald. — 1st ed.
p. cm.
Summary: Dual perspectives reveal the aftermath of seventeen-year-old Michael MacKenzie's birthday celebration during which he discharges an antique Winchester rifle and unknowingly kills the father of high school classmate Jenna Ward.
ISBN 978-0-385-32309-3 (hc) — ISBN 978-0-440-22672-7 (pbk.)
[1. Guilt—Fiction. 2. Death—Fiction. 3. Grief—Fiction. 4. Family life—Fiction.]
I. Title.
PZ7.M478418 Sw 1997
[Fic]—dc22
97001402

ISBN 978-0-307-97609-3 (trade pbk.)

RL: 5.7

Printed in the United States of America

10 9 8 7 6 5 4 3 2

First Ember Edition 2012

For my mother,
Mayme Elizabeth Schanbacher,
and
for Pamela Curtis Swallow

acknowledgments

For their helpful comments, support, and encouragement, I would like to thank Eugene Schanbacher; Dwaine McDonald; Kathryn Moody; Jack, Joni, John, and Jaime Schanbacher; the members of my writers' group; my agent, Renée Cho; and above all my editor, Lauri Hornik, for her generous inspiration and expert direction.

prologue

There is no stopping it; the bullet rips through the hot summer haze, missing trees, houses, unsuspecting birds, coming to roost, finally, like an old homing pigeon.

Jenna Ward's hand hangs above her brow, a visor blotting out the sun. Above her, on the roof, her father squeezes the steel staple gun, aiming for the shingle beneath his fingers. The sun ricochets off the shining steel, pelting Jenna's eyes. She can barely make out her father's face. He is a dark shadow, moving about clumsily like a squatting troll traversing rooftops.

For a single moment the sun dips behind a cloud. Jenna drops her hand from her forehead. Her father lifts his hand to wave, but it flops suddenly, the knuckles thudding against the new shingles. His eyes widen like dark coals; his mouth falls open, a silent black zero. Slowly his body folds over itself, and over, plunging to the porch roof below, rolling like a heavy log over the side, coming to rest, finally, by Jenna's bare feet.

Somewhere on the other side of Briarwood, over a mile away, in the woods behind his house, Michael MacKenzie gently strokes the silky stock of his .45-70 Winchester rifle while he holds it out for Joe Sadowski's admiration. And because he could not wait to feel the smooth curve of the trigger beneath his finger, he has fired one shot into the air. It is the Fourth of July, Michael's seventeenth birthday, and the rifle is a gift from his grandfather. His parents are throwing an all-day barbecue and pool party to celebrate. Before the sun sets, he will eat six hot dogs, four hamburgers, and a half pound of potato salad; he will sneak into the garage with Amy Ruggerio—even though his girlfriend, Darcy, is at the party—because Amy is a "babe" and wants him; he will drive the neighbors crazy with heavy metal blasting from his stereo. He will, in fact, think this is the best day of his life, because in that moment he does not know that he has accidentally killed a man.

michael

ichael MacKenzie had been awake since four that morning. His heart was pounding even faster than when he took his position at a track meet, waiting for the starter's "go." Finally, after what had seemed the longest year of his life, he would have wheels. Wheels and all the good things that went with them. The possibilities swarmed like bees inside his head.

He had been driving on his permit for the past year, had taken the driver's ed course at school, and now, one day after his seventeenth birthday, he would take his driver's test. By noon he'd be a free man, free to go where he wanted, free to cruise without another licensed driver in the car. A free man with wheels—even if they were his dad's. There wasn't anything better on this earth.

By six the sun had begun to spread its orange glow over the treetops. Michael swung his feet to the floor, absentmindedly combed his dark hair with his fingers, then reached to the foot of the bed, where he had tossed his cutoffs the previous night. Suddenly he was reminded of Amy Ruggerio and their sweaty ten minutes in the garage the day before. Darcy had been helping his mom with the potato salad. She hadn't suspected a thing.

He told himself Amy Ruggerio was easy, because that was what everyone said. And she had proved it, hadn't she? But that didn't change the urgent desire that rippled unexpectedly through his stomach and beyond. He could not shake the image of Amy's sad brown eyes, her smooth hand on his cheek as she looked up at him. It wasn't as if they'd really done anything. Just made out.

Still, there was that thing with her bikini top. He had accidentally torn one of the straps. He couldn't even remember how it happened. But Amy hadn't said a word. She'd just knotted it around the thin strip of material that tied in the back. Such a simple thing, but it made her seem so vulnerable. He had said he was sorry. And he was. She had smiled and said it was okay, she'd fix it later. But somehow it didn't seem okay. He wished he hadn't gone into the garage with her in the first place. He should have stayed with Darcy.

He shot one leg into his cutoffs, then the other. Why was he thinking about Amy Ruggerio anyway, especially today? He had better things to think about, like getting his license.

By six-thirty he had bolted down two blueberry Pop-Tarts and a glass of orange juice and was headed over to Joe Sadowski's. Joe was the only one of his friends who had his own car, a Mustang, fire-engine red with mag wheels. And he was letting Michael take his driver's test with it. Michael's dad had offered to go with him, had even offered him the family Honda Accord. But Michael explained that he'd already made other arrangements. Not that he minded his dad going with him. He didn't. It just looked better to go with a friend.

Joe was still in bed. So was everyone else in the family, except for Mr. Sadowski, who was getting ready for work and who showed up at the front door, towel in hand, with his flannel robe clinging to his dripping wet body. He stared at Michael as if the boy were a door-to-door salesman he was about to shout down.

"Joe ready?" Michael fisted his hands in his pockets, trying to look casual.

"It isn't even seven o'clock." Mr. Sadowski rubbed the bald spot on the top of his head with the towel. It gleamed a polished pink in the morning sunlight. "He doesn't usually get out of bed till noon when he has to go to work."

Joe worked at Burger King. It was a year-round job, although he put in longer hours in the summer, working afternoons and evenings. During the school year he worked only late afternoons and Saturdays. That was how he paid for his car insurance and gas.

"I know," Michael explained. "But I've got my driver's test this morning. He's going with me."

Mr. Sadowski seemed to consider this. Finally he stepped aside and cocked his head toward the stairs. "Good luck getting him up."

A moment later Michael stood over Joe's bed, studying him. Joe had kicked off the covers. His knees were drawn up to his chest, as if he couldn't get warm enough. He wore only black briefs, and his skin was puckered with goose bumps, even though it was already seventy-five degrees outside. Michael fought off a sudden urge to pull the top sheet over him.

"Hey, man," he said, giving Joe's shoulder a slight punch. Joe rolled over to his other side and pulled his knees deeper into his chest. Michael clamped his hand on Joe's shoulder again and rocked him back and forth.

Joe blinked twice and closed his eyes. "What the hell do you think you're doing?" he mumbled. His tongue was still swollen with sleep.

"We've got to be at the DMV by nine," Michael said.

Joe opened one eye and glanced at the window. "What time is it?"

Michael cleared his throat. "I thought you'd need some time to get ready, eat breakfast maybe."

Joe reached for the digital alarm clock. The bright blue numbers flashed 6:54. "Oh, man." He lifted one leg and booted Michael in the stomach with his foot, sending him up against the wall. "You're crazy, man. You know that?"

Still, by eight-thirty the two of them were on their way to the Division of Motor Vehicles. Heavy metal blasted from the car's speakers, drowning out everything else, cocooning them in the throbbing, pulsating bass that seemed to come from the gas pedal. The music climbed Michael's leg and flooded his belly with sound. He beat his hands on the steering wheel in time to the rhythm.

They had decided Michael would drive the car. He wanted to memorize the feel of the steering wheel, the amount of pressure needed on the brakes to bring the car to a slow, easy stop. As they cruised through town he decided to practice parallel parking one more time, although he'd done it hundreds of times over the past year.

Michael pulled up next to a beat-up blue Citation. Neither of the boys noticed that the music on the radio had stopped. A commercial for radial tires squawked out at them, followed by a brief traffic report. Michael put the car in reverse and began slowly backing up, careful to turn the wheel enough to angle the back end of the car into the empty space. The front of the car was still in the middle of the street when he felt Joe's hand on his wrist. The pressure of his friend's fingers burned into his skin. Joe was staring down at the radio as if it were a time bomb about to explode.

"What?" Michael asked.

"Shut up," Joe said, his voice a low, raspy whisper. "Listen."

The news reporter's voice was as smooth and even as a freshly planed board as he talked about the bizarre death on the Fourth of July of a man from Briarwood, New Jersey. The man had been repairing shingles on his roof around noon when a bullet from nowhere had dropped from the sky and killed him instantly. The reporter concluded by making an appeal to anyone in the area who might have information that would help the local police solve the case.

Michael never finished parking the car. In fact, he was a mile down the road, heading no place in particular, before he realized he was still behind the wheel and presumably in control. Neither of the boys spoke for several minutes. Joe never bothered to tell Michael he was headed in the opposite direction from the DMV.

When Joe finally did speak, he said, "It could have come from anywhere. It could have been anyone."

Michael's hands were so wet he was barely able to hold the steering wheel. He wanted to believe his friend. Joe was right. Lots of people had been shooting off firecrackers the day before. Probably shooting guns, too. Especially if they couldn't get their hands on a few packages of illegal fireworks. Anything to make noise. That's what the Fourth was about, right? Making a lot of noise. Guns probably had been going off all over the place.

Michael squeezed his eyes shut, as if he were fighting off a headache. Who was he kidding? The reporter had said it had happened around noon. That was when Michael had been showing off the Winchester to Joe. He looked over at his friend, saw the limp dirty-blond waves of his shoulder-length hair brush his pale cheek as he stared down at the floor, and he knew Joe was thinking the same thing.

"I shot it into the air," Michael said, scarcely able to breathe. "In the air, man. The bullet wasn't supposed to go anyplace." He pulled the car over to the shoulder and stopped. He did not trust himself to drive. Joe looked at him and shook his head. Michael couldn't tell whether he was disagreeing with him about the shooting or saying he didn't want to drive either.

The two of them sat in the car, letting the sun bake them through the roof. It never occurred to Michael to turn the engine back on so that they'd at least have air-conditioning.

Finally Joe pulled himself up straight and brushed his damp hair behind his ears. A single gold earring in the shape of a skull dangled from his earlobe. He grabbed Michael's upper arm as he might have grabbed the arm of a drowning man. "Listen," he said, leaning forward, "it was an accident."

"But it's still manslaughter, right? You could go to prison for something like that, right?"

"I don't know. Maybe." Joe shifted his gaze away from Michael's eyes. "Anyway, I think when it's an accident it's called involuntary manslaughter or something like that." He tightened his grip. "Look, nobody has to find out. Not if you get rid of the gun."

Michael felt the crablike pinch of Joe's fingers digging into his bare flesh. He yanked his arm away. "I'll know," he said.

"Get serious, man. Even if they don't send you to prison, think how this is going to look on your record. You can kiss off all those fancy colleges you were thinking of applying to."

Michael thought about the stack of university catalogs and applications on his desk at home. He might not have been Ivy League material, but he was counting on going to a good school, Lehigh maybe, or Lafayette. The full impact of what Joe had just said was beginning to sink in. This was his future they were talking about, everything Michael had been working for.

"There's some things you just got to live with," Joe was saying. "Things you do. You know? Stuff you don't want anybody to know about."

Michael looked over at his friend. He'd known Joe since second grade. They'd been best friends all these years, even though they were as different as night and day. He also knew he was Joe's only real friend. Most of the other kids at school had more or less written Joe off back in eighth grade when he'd been caught smashing roadside mailboxes with a baseball bat at one o'clock in the morning, drunk.

But no matter what kind of trouble Joe got into over the years, Michael still believed he was basically a decent person. And, even more important, he was the most loyal friend Michael had ever had.

Michael licked his lips. They were dry and tasted like salt. "Yeah, well, what would you know about it?"

"Come on, man. I've done things I ain't proud of. Nobody knows that better than you." Joe nodded slowly, his eyes narrowing to dark slits. "You just live with it, that's all."

But Joe was wrong. Michael knew he couldn't live with this. How could anybody live with this? Joe was watching him carefully, as if he expected him to suddenly lunge from the car into oncoming traffic.

"Anyway," Joe said, "we can't be sure. That bullet would've had to travel over a mile." He wiped the sweat from his face with his Woodstock II T-shirt. "Doesn't seem possible, you know? It would've hit a tree or something before it got that far."

Michael wanted to believe him, but something in his gut told him otherwise. What were the odds that someone else had fired a gun into the air right around noon? He knew what he'd done. He knew that a bullet, unobstructed, could travel as far as a mile before it finally headed back toward the earth. His stomach was churning violently. With one swift movement, he flung the door open, leaned over the side, and vomited.

Joe slid further down in his seat. He covered his eyes with his hand and shook his head. "We got to make a pact," he said as Michael let his head flop back against the headrest. When Michael didn't respond, he said, "Neither of us says anything, okay? I mean, I was there, remember. I was a witness. And if I don't come forward, that makes me an accessory to the crime. I'm in just as deep as you, man. But I'm not about to help you screw up your future."

Michael was only half listening. He felt as if his insides had been drained from him, as if he'd been stuffed with cotton. He did not trust himself to speak.

"Are you listening?" Joe said. "Because we got to act like nothing's happened. We got to turn this car around, and you got to take your driver's test just like everybody expects." He slapped the door handle with his hand, kicked the door open, and came around to the driver's side. "Move over." He shoved Michael's shoulder. "Get over," he said, pushing him to the passenger side. Then he slid behind the wheel and drove them to the DMV.

Later Michael hardly remembered the driver's test, remembered only how he'd felt as if he'd left his whole future sitting back there on the shoulder of the road. And when the man who gave him the test told him to turn right, Michael thought of all the years he had spent becoming the best track star Briarwood Regional had ever had. And he thought about the college applications he was planning to fill out.

When the man told him to do a three-point turn, Michael

carefully put the car in reverse and thought about his parents and his younger brother, Josh. What would they do if they knew they were harboring a killer under their roof? For that was what he was, right? A murderer. He tried to let the word penetrate, but it lay like a lump of lead, silent and unspoken, on his tongue. Accident or not, he had taken another person's life.

And when the man told him to drive down the block and turn left at the stop sign, Michael thought, for some crazy reason, about Amy Ruggerio and her torn bikini top, and suddenly he wanted to cry.

He did not pass his driver's test. He would have to try again later. He did not pass, because when the man told him to pull up next to the orange cones and then parallel park, Michael found he could not think clearly. His eyes burned so badly he couldn't see. His hands shook so much that he could not hold the steering wheel. Desperate, he reached for the key, shut off the engine, and climbed out of the car, leaving the keys in the ignition. The man, wearing a short-sleeved white shirt but no jacket, had loosened his tie and stared through the window at Michael, who had simply turned and walked away.

Later that day Michael went to a hardware store and bought a three-and-a-half-foot piece of PVC pipe and two end caps. That night, while the rest of his family slept, he put the Winchester inside the pipe, sealed the two end caps to keep water from getting in, carefully unstacked the firewood from the pile behind the garage, dug a three-foot-deep trench, buried the rifle, and restacked the wood. Then he went to bed and lay awake the entire night, wondering if he would ever sleep again.

jenna

2

Charlie Ward's death made the national news only hours after it had happened, although few people noticed. They were too caught up in watching the brilliant dazzle of color exploding above them in celebration of Independence Day. The anchorman on one major network called Charlie Ward's death a "bizarre accident"; another referred to it as a "rain of death from the sky." But Jenna Ward did not watch the news that night. Fred Campbell, the family's physician, concerned about the effect that the barrage of firecrackers and cherry bombs in the neighborhood would have on Jenna and her mother, had given them each a sedative and sent them to bed. They had slept through the entire night, unaware of the reporters stalking below their bedroom windows.

The Briarwood police had cordoned off the area, stretching yellow tape across the front yard to ward off morbid spectators. Dave Zelenski, the local police chief, had stationed police officers round the clock at the scene of the accident. And so it was that Jenna, her head dulled from the aftermath of the sedative, peered out her bedroom window on the following morning to see a police officer standing at the end of her driveway. That was how she knew the nightmare of the day before had really happened.

Outside, the July sun was just spilling over the rooftop of the church across the street. Without checking her clock, Jenna knew it was early, probably no later than six. As she watched the police officer take a Thermos from his car and pour himself a cup of coffee, she wondered what she should be feeling. Because the truth was, she felt nothing.

Below, on the roof of the front porch, a tight line of mourning doves had gathered. They sat as rigid as little gray soldiers, their feathers pressed so close together that Jenna thought if one flew off, they would all be lifted into the air in a long silver rope of birds.

For a long time she watched the birds, because she did not know what else to do. Then she rummaged through one of the drawers for a pair of shorts and a top, dressed indifferently, and wandered into the bathroom to brush her teeth.

She splashed cold water on her face and reached for a towel. The unmistakable scent of her father's Royal Copenhagen aftershave rushed up to greet her. He had used this towel, probably only the day before. She held the towel in her hand for a few minutes, then folded it neatly and hung it on the rack, as if she were expecting him to use it later.

Barefoot, her dark blond hair still a tangled mess, she descended the stairs. The house seemed unusually large and silent. But it smelled the same: an odor of rose-petal potpourri, strategically placed in bowls and baskets in every room by her mother. The odor had never seemed so overpowering before. It made her gag.

The kitchen was no better, so she took the basket of rose petals from its place on the counter and dumped the contents into the trash compactor. Her mother would be furious. Jenna shrugged at the thought. So what else was new?

She reached for the teakettle, filled it with water, and put it on to boil. It was all so odd, she thought. Here she was, calmly going about her morning routine as if nothing had changed. She felt as if she were standing outside herself, watching as she opened the small white envelope and pulled out the tea bag. Watching as she set it in a mug. Watching for her hand to shake, which it never did. Not so much as a tremor. She poured the boiling water and added a packet of sugar substitute, all very matter-of-factly.

While she waited for the tea to steep, she studied the list of chores that her mother had made up for her father and taped to the refrigerator door. The list was an old joke between her parents. Her father had called it the "Honey Do" list. At the top of the list, underlined twice, was PATCH LEAK IN ROOF. Jenna lifted the magnetic pencil from the door and crossed off that first item.

When her tea was ready, she picked up the mug and carried it down to the basement. In the far corner was her father's workshop. She knew she had come here on purpose. The smell of sawdust was as powerful a reminder as his aftershave. She set the mug on the workbench and positioned herself on his stool. The metal rung bit into the arches of her bare feet.

She looked around the workshop. This had been her father's sacred place. He had loved nothing better than to spend a few hours on weekends building things.

Jenna lifted a hammer from the bench, turning it over and over in her hand, feeling its weight. Her father had never spent as much time down here as he'd wanted. His life had been an endless round of meetings and negotiations. He had been in upper management at AT&T for as long as she could remember.

She set the hammer down, reached for her mug of tea, and blew into the rising steam. Usually her father would be halfway to his office by now. And in some strange way it seemed as if he *were* on his way to work, just like any other day. At six o'clock that evening or thereabouts, he would come bounding through the front door, fly up the stairs, grab his swim trunks, and make a mad dash for the pool in the back-yard, just as he had done every night in the summer. That was the reality. It had always been the reality.

Jenna could not make herself believe otherwise. Yes, the ambulance had come. Yes, the attendants had strapped her father to a gurney. And yes, the blood from the wound in the back of his head had leaked onto the white sheet. But that didn't mean he was dead, did it?

She stared down at the floor. Small piles of sawdust littered the area like anthills. Her father rarely had bothered to sweep it up. He'd liked it on the floor. She dug into one of the piles with her big toe, suddenly aware that she had her ear cocked toward the staircase, listening for her father's footsteps.

But when the footsteps came, they were lighter, quicker, and Jenna knew that her mother was overhead in the kitchen. The basement door clicked open.

"Jenna, are you down there?" Her mother's voice was like the crash of cymbals coming at the end of a lullaby. It was always like that these days. Jenna's body grew rigid, a simple reflex action. She sat silent and motionless.

"I need you up here." There was a brief pause. "Now." Couldn't her mother leave her alone for even a minute? Just a few minutes alone to try to understand this terrible thing that was happening to them?

Jenna took a swallow of her tea and tried to remember if she was even talking to her mother this week. They had had so many fights over the past few years, spent so many weeks barely speaking to each other, that she found it hard to keep track.

She stared down at the mug in her hand. The tea had become lukewarm. She shouldn't be behaving like this. She had lost her father. Her mother had lost her husband. They should be trying to comfort each other, not bite each other's heads off.

Reluctantly she slid off the stool and padded up the stairs to the kitchen, where she found her mother, a bottle of Fantastik in one hand and a wad of paper towels in the other, frantically wiping down the stove. Her mother nodded toward the vacuum cleaner in the dining room.

Jenna blinked but did not move. Surely her mother didn't expect her to vacuum the carpet.

Meredith Ward tossed the clump of soggy paper towels into the trash compactor and pulled another handful from the roll next to the sink.

"Mom . . ." Jenna found she could not finish her thought, because she didn't know what it was she wanted to say.

Her mother was staring down at the bottle of Fantastik in her hand as if she were trying to remember where it had come from. She set the container on the counter, wiped her hands on her yellow shorts, and tucked the loose strands of her hair— hair much like Jenna's, only shorter—back into the wide barrette at the nape of her neck. Then she poured herself a cup of coffee.

"People will be coming to the house," she said. "We have

to get organized." She looked over the rim of her coffee mug at her daughter's face, closed her eyes, and breathed deeply. "I'm sorry, Jen. I wish I knew a way to make this easier for you. For both of us. But I don't." She set the mug back on the counter without taking a swallow. "We have to get through this somehow. People will be coming to the house, and it's a mess. I'm counting on you."

Jenna stared over at the vacuum cleaner. Suddenly it was just like any other morning. Especially those Saturday mornings when she wanted to go to the mall with her friends and her mother insisted she stay home and help her with the housework. Those Saturday mornings almost always ended in a screaming match.

"Nobody's going to care if the house is a mess." Jenna sucked in the sides of her mouth, a habit she had acquired as a small child when she was upset. Then, as if she needed to test the words, she whispered, "Good Lord, Mom, Daddy's dead." She waited to see if saying this out loud would somehow make it more real. It didn't. "Nobody's going to notice lint on the carpet."

Their eyes locked. Her mother seemed to be holding her breath. Then, without a word, she grabbed a bottle of Soft Scrub from under the sink and left the room. That was when Jenna understood that her mother did not believe what was happening to them any more than she did.

Jenna sat down cross-legged on the floor next to the vacuum cleaner, her hand resting on the cool plastic as if she were stroking a family pet. Well, fine. Her mother could Soft Scrub the bathroom tiles until her fingers bled, but Jenna would not be a part of it.

In the end, though, Jenna vacuumed not only every rug in the house but all the upholstered furniture and all the bedspreads and drapes. The work kept her busy, and she didn't have to think, which, much as she hated to admit it, might have been just what her mother had in mind. By the time Chief Zelenski arrived to take their statements, the house was spotless.

The police were the only people her mother allowed in the house that morning, except for Mr. Krebs, the widower from next door, who, although almost eighty, kept the reporters at bay like a loyal palace guard, screened telephone calls, and took messages.

An autopsy had been done only hours after what everyone kept calling "the accident," but Chief Zelenski would not reveal the findings, explaining that giving out any information would interfere with the investigation. Jenna stubbornly refused to accept that this was just some accident. This was a murder. Her father was dead. And somebody was going to have to pay for it.

She slid her hands under her thighs to warm her fingers. The room was ice-cold. Her mother always kept the central air-conditioning running. Jenna hated having the house all closed up in the summer.

She looked over at Dave Zelenski, who sat in the chair next to her. He was a middle-aged man with a robust, ruddy face and wire-rimmed glasses that seemed to be constantly sliding down his nose, no matter how many times he pushed them back in place. Under different circumstances, she would have found this funny.

"I know this is difficult for you, Mrs. Ward," he told Jenna's mother, looking slightly embarrassed. "But I need you to tell me everything that happened yesterday."

Jenna glanced across the room to where her mother sat on the couch, looking calm and composed. Meredith Ward had changed from her shorts into a sleeveless sundress. The sheer fabric with tiny pastel flowers fell in soft folds about her ankles. Jenna's hand went instinctively to the side of her head. She suddenly remembered that she still had not combed her hair. Her mother was watching her. She attempted to give her daughter a reassuring nod, but Jenna pretended not to notice.

She scarcely listened as Chief Zelenski began asking her mother questions. When he finally turned to Jenna, she slowly and methodically related what she could remember from that day. Images flooded her mind, images of her father lying at her feet; of the staple gun, still on the roof where he had dropped it, glinting in the sharp noonday sun; of her mother running from the house, drawn by her daughter's unbearable screams, running toward her, balancing a plate with a tuna fish sandwich, unaware that she had it in her hand. But these were the only images that came to mind. The rest of the morning was a blank.

"Can you remember anything else?" Chief Zelenski asked. He raised his eyebrows, and as he did, his glasses once again slid down his nose. This time he took them off and slipped them into his shirt pocket. "I know it's hard, but—"

"How would you know?" Jenna said. She wasn't trying to be rude. She simply hated it when people assumed they knew what she was feeling. Especially now, when it bothered her that she wasn't feeling much of anything at all.

Chief Zelenski stared at Jenna as if he thought she was intentionally trying to impede his investigation. But he said nothing. Instead he began to drone on about how the local ballistics team didn't have the knowledge or the equipment to figure the trajectory of the bullet. So they were going to turn it over to the experts, engineers from Picatinny Arsenal, who could figure the coordinates on their computer. They could, according to Chief Zelenski, determine the arc of the bullet from the point of impact all the way back to where the gun had been fired. But, he explained, looking apologetic, the men from Picatinny were in the middle of another project and wouldn't be available for a while.

"A while?" Meredith Ward asked. "What does that mean? Two days? Two years?" Her mother's voice, usually even and controlled, wavered slightly. Jenna studied her mother closely, watching for other signs that there might be a crack in her professional veneer.

Meredith Ward was an account executive for a large New York advertising agency. She was not a person to be kept waiting. Jenna knew this from experience. She had seen her mother hang up the phone dozens of times just because someone had dared to put her on hold. To hear her mother's voice quake, even slightly, was disturbing.

Dave Zelenski shifted uneasily in his chair and ran his palm across his thinning hair. "Hard to say. These guys can be unpredictable."

Jenna rose abruptly. She stared down at the police chief. "So was the lunatic who shot my father."

"It's okay." Meredith Ward crossed the room and put an arm around her daughter's shoulder.

Jenna pulled away from her. "What's okay?" She narrowed her eyes at her mother. "What are you talking about? Nothing's 'okay.' Nothing will ever be 'okay' again." Each time she emphasized the word *okay* she sounded as if she were trying to take a bite out of it.

Her mother shook her head. "I was talking about the investigation," she said, ignoring Jenna's outburst. "I meant sometimes these things take time, even if we'd like them to go a lot faster." Her mother's composure only infuriated Jenna all the more.

"Well, I can tell you this, anyway," Chief Zelenski said, looking relieved that he could offer them something. "One of their guys will be out here tomorrow to start collecting information from the site. They'll probably want to go over the police report then, too."

Meredith Ward began to massage the space between her eyebrows with her thumb and forefinger. She looked over at Jenna. She seemed to be waiting for something.

Jenna thought that if she stayed in the room another minute, she would suffocate. All she wanted to do was get out of there. Without another word, she headed for the front foyer. She would take a walk, and when she came back, everything would magically be just as it had been before the accident. Her father would be there, and Chief Zelenski and this whole horrible nightmare would have disappeared.

But when she opened the front door, she found herself right in the line of fire, assaulted on all sides by a barrage of reporters and photographers. Too shocked by the intrusion to react, she merely pulled back into the foyer, like a turtle seeking the safety of its shell. Then she sat down on the stairs, folded her head into her lap, and waited for the tears that would not come.

michael

michael waited until he heard his mom and dad leave for work before he kicked back the covers and headed downstairs. He knew his brother, Josh, usually slept late. Thankfully, Michael found himself alone. No one was there to ask about the dark circles beneath his eyes or why he couldn't seem to form a coherent sentence.

Someone, probably his father, had left an open carton of milk and an empty cereal bowl on the table. Michael absentmindedly put the milk back in the refrigerator and the bowl in the sink. Cleaning up after his family, or after himself for that matter, was not something he normally did. But then, nothing about him felt normal.

He toasted a bagel, buttered it, and slid it onto the table, not bothering with a plate. As he was about to sit down he noticed the morning newspaper, which had been left on the chair. A face stared up at him from the front page, a young face with enormous sad eyes. The girl's hair, shoulder length and straight, was parted in the middle, with one side pushed behind her ear; the other side hung loosely against her cheek. The headline read "Briarwood Man's Death Still a Mystery." It took only a glance at the article for Michael to realize he had been looking at the face of the dead man's daughter. Her name was Jenna Ward. And although the family had not given any statements to the press and had asked to be left alone to grieve in peace, apparently a persistent photographer with a telephoto lens had somehow managed to snap this picture.

Michael tossed the paper on the table and sat down, bracing his head with his hands. He did not want to read the article. He did not want to know anything about these people. But he could not seem to keep his eyes from gobbling up every word, even though his mind screamed in protest.

It was all there, every detail that had so far been disclosed, just as the reporter on the radio had related it the day before. Michael's head dropped forward, and it was only minutes later that he realized his forehead had been pressing against the forehead in the picture. The ink left a dark smudge on his skin, like ashes on Ash Wednesday.

He wanted to say something to her, something to take the pain from those sad eyes. How it had been an accident. That he wasn't a murderer. That he could never kill anyone. How even after his grandfather had given him the antique Winchester (which had been his when he was a boy), he knew he'd never use it to hurt anything. He wanted to tell her how he planned to use it just for target practice at the range. But all that seemed so meaningless. He'd killed her father, for god's sake. Did he think for a second she'd give a damn how bad he felt?

Suddenly he became aware of the sound of cabinet doors being opened and closed. Michael drew his eyes away from the picture in the newspaper and came face-to-face with Josh. He hadn't even heard him come in.

His brother stood there in baggy shorts and a dirty T-shirt. He wore his baseball cap backward, covering most of his unruly hair. Still, an obstinate clump had managed to escape through the open space above the band. At thirteen, Josh tended to swing back and forth between outrageous comic antics and moody sullenness. No one in the family knew what to expect from him anymore.

Josh stared at his older brother for a minute, then reached for the carton of orange juice in the refrigerator. Neither boy spoke.

Then he sat down across from Michael and began drinking the orange juice right from the container.

"Other people live in this house," Michael reminded him.

Josh slammed the carton onto the table and gave him a satisfied grin. Orange juice dribbled down his chin.

He knew Josh was just trying to get a rise out of him. Michael shoved the newspaper to one side and stood up.

Josh leaned across the table on his elbows. "Hey," he said, poking his finger into the face of Jenna Ward, "that's that guy's kid. You know, that guy who got shot on his roof two days ago." His eyes widened. "Cool!"

Michael stared down at his uneaten bagel. The excited, almost gleeful expression on Josh's face horrified him. "What would you know about it?" he said, straining to keep his voice flat and even.

Josh's eyebrows shot up in amazement. "You're kidding, right? Everybody in town knows about it. That's all anybody talked about around here yesterday."

Michael had managed to successfully avoid almost everybody the day before. After he had left the DMV, having refused Joe's offer to drive him home, he had hopped a local bus with no intention of going anywhere in particular. He had just wanted to get away. For a brief while, he had thought about taking the bus to Newark, then catching another bus out of the state. But that had seemed like a dumb idea. It would have only pointed the finger right at him.

Instead he had ended up two towns away, hung out at a mall until after dinner, and finally bought the PVC pipe before heading home. All his father had said, when Michael came through the living room after burying the rifle, was, "Out celebrating with Joe, huh? Big day, getting your license."

Michael had not expected to find his father still up. It was past midnight, and he had thought everyone was in bed. He wondered if his father had heard him in the basement getting the rifle from the gun cabinet. Managing a strained smile, he mumbled, "Yeah," then headed for the stairs.

"Well, come on," his father said. "Let's hear about it."

Michael stopped halfway up the stairs. His hand reached for the banister. "What's to hear? It was a driver's test, Dad."

His father pulled the car keys from his pants pocket. "Want to take her around the block a few times?"

What could he say? *Sorry, Dad, I didn't pass the test because I just found out I might have killed a man. So you'll have to excuse me if I don't take you up on your offer.* Michael pretended to stifle a yawn and told his father he was pretty beat. "Besides," he said, "I've been driving all day." Then he had headed up to his room.

Josh leaned across the newspaper; his face was only inches from Michael's. "Who do you think did it? Somebody from around here?"

"Who knows?" Michael glanced up at the clock. It was past eight-thirty. He had to be on duty at the pool by nine. "I'm gonna be late," he said, heading for the back door.

"Hey," Josh shouted after him. "What about that gun

Grandpa gave you?" His laugh came out in little snorts. "Done any shooting lately?"

Michael was already halfway down the walk and pretended not to hear. He knew Josh was still trying to get to him.

When he got to the end of the walk he stopped, realizing suddenly that the last place he felt like going was to work. He thought about calling in sick, then immediately abandoned the idea. The only reason Simon Goldfarb had given him two days off in the first place was because Mr. Goldfarb was a close friend of his dad's. Never in a million years would Mr. Goldfarb have allowed any other lifeguard to take off the Fourth of July, the busiest day of the summer, let alone the day after so that he could go for his driver's test. The two days off had been his birthday present to Michael.

He slowed his pace, stalling for time. Maybe he just wouldn't show up for work. It wasn't as if he were the only lifeguard; there were five others. But then, where would he go? Reluctantly he continued in the direction of the Briarwood Community Pool.

From the moment Michael walked through the front gate, he was surrounded by friends who wanted to talk about his party. So far they had rated it the best party of the summer, an honor Michael chose not to take seriously, considering school had been out for only two weeks. In fact, he wanted nothing more than to forget the stupid party.

It was ninety-two degrees outside, and the pool was mobbed. As he climbed onto the lifeguard stand Michael wondered how he was going to keep an eye on all the people in his section. Packed together like bowling pins, they bobbed about, diving underwater, jumping on each other's shoulders, cannonballing off the side of the pool, splashing wet chaos everywhere.

Michael adjusted his sunglasses and smeared thick white ointment on his nose and lips. Two sophomore girls from his high school wandered up to his stand and stood below, talking about some party they had been to the night before. They hovered inches from his feet, wringing out their wet hair and laughing. He was used to this. Girls of all ages constantly hung around the male lifeguards' stands, even though there were signs all over the place saying not to distract the guards from their duty. Ordinarily he would have eaten this up, but today he just wanted them to go away, take their adolescent giggling and their long wet hair and their suntanned bodies someplace else.

"What happened to you guys yesterday?" The voice floated up to him from below. He didn't have to look to know it belonged to Darcy Kelly. He glanced over his shoulder and saw her leaning against the back of the stand, arms folded. She did not look up. Her wet dark red hair hung about her shoulders like water snakes. When Michael didn't say anything, Darcy continued her monologue, seemingly to no one in particular.

"A person waits all afternoon because she's supposed to be the first to ride with her boyfriend after he gets his license. Only he never shows." She wandered around to the front of the stand, arms still folded. The two sophomores, sensing trouble, quickly made their way over to the other side of the pool. "So, what do you make of that?" Darcy asked, shading her eyes with her hand as she glared up at him.

Michael noticed that she was wearing the one-piece bathing suit with the bright orange flowers all over it. His favorite. He swallowed hard. He did not know what to say. The truth was, he hadn't thought about Darcy at all since yesterday morning. He had completely forgotten he'd promised her a ride in Joe's car.

"Hel-*lo-o-o*," she called, as if she were shouting down a wind tunnel. "Anybody home up there?"

Michael shifted in his seat, trying to find a comfortable spot, which under the circumstances was impossible. Finally he managed to mumble, "I'm sorry. I forgot, that's all."

"That's all?" Darcy snapped her fingers. "Just like that?"

Because he didn't want to have to explain anything more, he said, "Darcy, later, okay? You know the rules around here. Do you want me to lose my job?"

"Your job?" she said, letting her smile slide into a half sneer. "Well, maybe there's more at stake here than your job." Then, as if realizing she had pushed things too far, she took a step back. "Okay, later." She turned to go, stopped, started again, then over her shoulder said casually, "Call me tonight. We'll talk."

Michael watched the gentle sway of her hips as she crossed over to where a group of her friends sat playing cards and drinking bottles of Snapple beneath a tree. Talk? What could they possibly have to talk about? Couldn't she see he wasn't the same person she'd been going out with for the past six months?

He knew he wasn't being fair to Darcy. He owed her something. But that something was an explanation, which was one thing he quite simply couldn't give her.

He felt the sudden bite of icy water on his feet and looked down to see two little girls, arms resting on the edge of the pool as their bodies bobbed back and forth in the water. He figured they were about ten. They giggled, then sent another splash of water in his direction. "Help, save me," one of them said, pushing herself away from the edge and pretending to go under. Her friend laughed hysterically, then did the same.

In the past he would have given them a warning, lectured them on the dangers of crying wolf, and made them stay out of the pool for the next half hour. But today he could only stare blankly at the girls. And the water they splashed on his skin seemed to sting like fire, because he was suddenly reminded of something that had happened to another girl about the same age several years before the community pool was built. Back then everyone went swimming in a nearby lake. Michael had been there that day. He remembered the lifeguards diving frantically beneath the water's surface, remembered one of them carrying out the limp body of the girl and laying her in the sand. They had worked on her for what seemed like hours, using cardiopulmonary resuscitation, using everything they had ever learned. But the child had died.

Later one of the girl's friends told the police they had been diving for stones, picking them up with their teeth, and bringing them to the surface. Hard-won trophies for their daring. When her friend didn't come up from her third dive, the child had run to the lifeguards for help. But it was already too late. A small stone had lodged in the girl's windpipe, choking her to death. Michael remembered thinking at the time that if she had only swallowed the stone, maybe she would have lived, but she had probably panicked and inhaled it.

That was the thing about finding a stone in your throat when it was too late to spit it out. If you panicked and tried to take a deep breath, it would cut off your air and you'd die. You had to make yourself swallow it. The stone would probably tear your gut apart, but you'd survive. You'd have a future.

And he still had his future. That was the important thing, wasn't it? He had done what he needed to do to survive.

The unrelenting bogus cries from the two little girls below tore at him. What made these people think he could save them? Who was he to save anybody? The huge sad eyes from the morning paper floated before him, and he squeezed his own eyes shut in defense.

When he finally opened them again, he realized he was staring right at Amy Ruggerio, although she wasn't aware of it. She had set her beach towel on the lawn on the other side of the pool, directly across from him. She was alone, as usual, and seemed preoccupied with putting a coat of polish on her fingernails. A soft cascade of dark brown hair hung in loose ripples along the sides of her face as she bent over her hand.

He realized that almost every time he saw Amy, she was smearing stuff on her face or spraying junk in her hair. She actually *made* herself look like a slut. He couldn't understand why. She was pretty enough. Not beautiful or anything. But she had a nice face. What he would call likable. Why was she always hiding it under a lot of goop?

As if she suddenly sensed his presence, Amy looked up, saw him across the pool, and waved. His instinct was to ignore her. He was wearing sunglasses. She wouldn't be able to tell if he saw her or not. But to his amazement he felt his hand, as if it had a mind all its own, jerk upward in an awkward gesture of acknowledgment.

ichael did not go right home after work. Instead he headed for the public library. For a while he sat on the stone steps watching a woman peel old posters from the window of the Taggart Travel Agency. It was far easier to sit there watching someone else than to do what he had come for, which was to read every article in every newspaper that even so much as mentioned the Ward case. Though part of him resisted—the part that kept him sitting on the front steps of the library—he told himself he had to keep on top of the case, one step ahead of the police. He had to know what they knew. It was a simple matter of survival. But he wasn't fooling himself. He knew he had come to the library to find out all he could about Jenna and her family. Not that he expected the newspapers to give a lot of personal information about them. But he didn't know anyone who knew the Wards, and he had no other way of finding out how they were doing.

He glanced down at his watch. Five-thirty. It was Thursday evening. The library would be open until eight. The woman was no longer in the window across the street. Not much else was going on. Nothing that he could use as an excuse. So he finally went inside, found the local newspaper from the previous day, and began to read. The headline on the front page loomed up at him: "Mystery Surrounds Briarwood Killing." The article made his blood run cold with its matter-of-factness. He read how Charlie Ward had been repairing his roof on the Fourth of July when a bullet dropped from the sky, piercing the back of his skull. He read how no one had any idea who killed the man, probably not even the killer himself. He read how ballistics tests were being conducted with the hope of identifying the weapon. Then the article went on to mention that Charlie Ward had been in top management at AT&T, that his wife was an account executive for some big advertising firm, and that he had a fifteen-year-old daughter. It was all so impersonal. But Michael kept on reading. And he did not stop until he had read every account in all of the papers for the past two days.

ichael's mother was just taking a chicken casserole from the microwave when he walked through the back door. Michael stared at her for a minute as if he couldn't quite understand what she was doing there.

Karen MacKenzie wiped a thin film of perspiration from her upper lip. "Good timing," she said, setting the covered dish on the table.

Since it was already a few minutes past seven, Michael had figured that everyone else would have already eaten dinner. In fact, he had been counting on it.

"Oh, Darcy called. She left a message on the answering machine, something about Steven Chang's party." She stood on tiptoe to reach the plates in the cabinet. "Maybe you should call her before we sit down to dinner," she said over her shoulder. "This thing's too hot to eat right now, anyway."

Michael had forgotten about the party. He wondered why

Darcy hadn't mentioned it at the pool that afternoon, why she had waited until she got home to call him, knowing that probably no one would be there. He continued to stare at his mother as she set the plates on the table. Her lightly freckled face and neck were covered with large red splotches. Her face always became blotchy in extreme heat. She shoved her short, damp hair away from her forehead with her arm. "What?"

Michael hadn't realized he'd been staring at her. He couldn't seem to think clearly. "Nothing," he said finally. "I guess I sort of forgot about the party."

"Well, then, you'd better go call." She looked sadly at the steaming casserole. "What was I thinking? It's too hot out to eat something like this."

Michael lifted the cordless phone from the kitchen wall and wandered into the living room.

From his favorite recliner—strategically parked in front of the TV—Tom MacKenzie shouted, "What is *The Exterminator*?"

Josh shot him an outraged look from his place on the floor, three feet from the TV screen. "No, Dad. What is *The Terminator*? *The Terminator*," he repeated for emphasis. The contestant on the screen echoed, "What is *The Terminator*?"

Michael felt the muscles in his neck tighten.

"See?" Josh said.

"I knew that." His father flopped back in his chair. "It just came out wrong."

"Yeah, tell that to Alex Trebek."

Michael watched as Josh and their father engaged in their nightly ritual. Josh had been planning for two years to win big bucks on *Jeopardy!* His father liked to think of himself as Josh's personal trainer, although Michael seriously doubted they even had such a thing for game-show contestants.

That was his dad for you. Whatever his sons aspired to, he was right behind them every step of the way. Michael sometimes wondered if maybe his father had his own unfulfilled dreams. Still, he seemed satisfied enough with his position as manager at the local A&P.

For a few minutes he stood beneath the archway that separated the dining room from the living room, watching Josh and his dad; then he took the cordless phone up to his room and dialed Darcy's number. He was certain that her afternoon message was her way of making sure he'd call her that evening.

But all she said was, "What time are you picking me up?"

The phone felt slippery in his hand. "I don't know. What time does the party start?" He couldn't believe he had said that. He no more wanted to go to this party than he wanted to go to Siberia. And at the moment Siberia didn't sound half bad.

"Eight, I think. Nobody'll be there till later." He could hear her soft breathing on the other end. "So I guess eight-thirty's good."

"I just got home," he explained, as if that made any difference.

Darcy didn't say anything for a while. Then she cleared her throat and said, "So you want to make it later?"

He didn't want to make it at all. "Eight-thirty's okay. I already took a shower at the pool."

"You okay?" she asked.

He tried for a casual chuckle, but it stuck in his throat. "Fine. Why?"

"Oh, nothing."

"See you at eight-thirty," he said, trying to put an end to the conversation. Then he hung up before she could ask any more questions.

ichael fished around with his fork for chunks of chicken in the clump of mushy noodles on his plate. Josh had already finished eating and was back in front of the TV, watching *Wheel of Fortune*. Tom MacKenzie helped himself to a can of beer from the refrigerator. He still had half a plateful of food. Only Josh—who, according to his father, had the appetite of a boa constrictor—had eaten everything.

Michael's mother looked at their plates and sighed apologetically. "I guess I overcooked the noodles."

Nobody said anything.

"Well, I wouldn't have been so late tonight except the shop was a madhouse today." Karen MacKenzie worked at Briarwood Florist. What had begun as a part-time morning job two years earlier had evolved into a full-time position. Michael and his father were used to her talking about the place being a madhouse, especially around holidays. But it wasn't a holiday.

Tom MacKenzie took a swallow of beer and frowned. "A madhouse? In July?"

Michael's mother began scraping the food from her plate into the trash compactor. "It's that Ward funeral. Everybody's sending flowers, even though the family specifically asked people to make donations to charity instead." She sighed. "Only nobody paid any attention, of course. So we're swamped."

Michael did not look up. He saw his mother's freckled hand slide deftly beneath his gaze and lift his plate. "Finished?" she asked.

He nodded, not trusting himself to speak.

"I read somewhere that he had a fifteen-year-old daughter. She probably goes to your school," his mother said, looking at Michael. "Do you know her?"

44

He shook his head. The chicken casserole turned over in his stomach. Why hadn't he thought of that? Jenna Ward probably did go to Briarwood Regional. After all, the family *was* from Briarwood, although they lived on the other side of town. He hadn't recognized her from the picture in the newspaper, so he'd been sure he had never seen her before. Now he began to worry about what he would do if he saw her in the halls in September.

"Such a terrible tragedy." Slowly his mother lowered herself back into her chair, looking thoughtful.

"A stupid tragedy." His father pounded his fist on the table. In spite of himself, Michael flinched. "That's what happens when irresponsible people play around with guns." His father squeezed Michael's shoulder. "That's why I've taught my boys to respect guns."

Michael felt the pressure of his father's fingers digging into his collarbone. He wondered if his parents could see that he was shaking. Slowly, using all the muscle control he could muster, he stood up. Praying his legs would not give out on him, he turned to leave. "Sorry," he said, "I've got to pick up Darcy."

"Got a date with Darcy?" his father said. "Well, why didn't you say so? Here."

Michael glanced back at his father and saw that he was holding up the car keys. He looked very pleased with himself.

Michael felt his face flush. What could he say? His father would never believe he'd pass up a chance to drive the car. So in the end Michael simply took the keys, thanked his father, and headed upstairs to change his shirt. He told himself this was just another stone he had to swallow, and a small one by comparison. What was driving without a license compared to killing a man?

A half hour later he was standing at Darcy's front door. Darcy looked beautiful. Her thick hair hung almost to her waist in tight little waves. She wore pale peach shorts with a flowered top. Michael blinked in admiration.

"You're actually on time," she said, stepping outside. Then she turned and shouted back through the front door that they were leaving for the party.

Michael was glad she was ready to go. The last thing he felt like doing was talking to her parents.

Darcy looked out at the road. "Hey, your dad let you have the car!"

"Yeah. Well, maybe by the end of the summer I'll have my own wheels." He said this because he thought it was expected. He'd been saving for a car for almost a year, and all his friends, including Darcy, knew it.

They drove toward Steven Chang's house just as the streetlights came on. The light filtered through the branches, spreading leafy patterns on the sidewalk and street. Darcy reached for his hand, and the gentle pressure of her soft skin hurt him in a way he had never known.

He wanted to say something to her. He had even rehearsed it in front of the bathroom mirror. He would tell her they were seeing too much of each other, that they should start dating other people. But now, sitting next to Darcy, it sounded so phony. Everyone said that kind of crap when they wanted to break up with somebody. And the truth was, he still cared about her. He just couldn't be with her right now. He couldn't be with anyone.

Steven Chang's house was only two blocks away. Michael could hear the music even before they turned onto Steven's street. He was relieved when they made it through the front door without ever exchanging a word. Darcy never even mentioned how he'd forgotten her the day before. He was sure, after the scene at the pool that afternoon, that she was planning to read him the riot act. But so far she hadn't said anything.

Once they were inside, Darcy left him while she went to talk to two of her girlfriends in the kitchen, saying she'd get him something to drink while she was out there. Michael watched her disappear into the other room. He liked to watch her leaving and entering rooms. She had the most graceful body he'd ever seen. She seemed so at home in it.

The room was wall-to-wall kids. Somebody put on a rap CD and turned the volume up full blast. The furniture had been pushed back so that people could dance.

The smoke in the room stung Michael's eyes. The music was already beginning to give him a headache. He scouted around for a place to sit, finally deciding on the stairs leading to the second floor. He sat on the bottom step, back braced against the wall.

Two girls stepped over him to go upstairs. Michael recognized them, although he did not know them well. Suddenly, unexpectedly, he heard Jenna Ward's name.

The taller of the two, a girl with tight cutoffs and straight blond hair, was going on about how sad it was, especially since Jenna Ward was a classmate of her younger sister. "Can you imagine how freaky that would have been?" she said to the other girl. "One minute you're talking to your father, who's up on the roof, and the next minute he's lying at your feet . . . dead." Their voices drifted off as they reached the top step and started down the hall.

Michael pressed his palms against his eyes. Hard. So Jenna had been there when it happened. She had seen everything. Why hadn't that been in the newspapers?

His first instinct was to bolt. He had to get out of there.

He would make up some excuse to tell Darcy later. He was so intent on planning his escape, he barely noticed that someone had tapped him on the shoulder.

He smelled her perfume before he actually heard her voice, her soft, throaty "Hi, Mike." Michael looked up and found himself staring right into Amy Ruggerio's brown eyes. They were heavily rimmed with black eyeliner. Even with the air-conditioning on, the room was unbearably hot. Amy's face was shiny with perspiration that had streaked her makeup.

Michael nodded but said nothing. He did not want her to sit down next to him. What if Darcy saw them together? Besides, all he wanted was to leave. He wondered if Amy was with someone or if she had just wandered into the party on her own.

He remembered how Joe Sadowski had shown up with her at Michael's birthday party a few days earlier and announced, when Amy was out of hearing distance, that he'd brought her for Michael. She was his birthday present, Joe told him. Joe usually referred to her as the pig, and he'd made it clear he wouldn't have been caught dead with Amy under any other circumstances. He seemed to think it was a pretty good joke, too, claiming that Amy was so dumb she actually thought he wanted to go out with her.

"Great party," Amy shouted above the music. She sat down on the next step up. Michael kept his attention focused on the kitchen door.

"Yeah."

"Not as good as yours, though."

Michael wished she hadn't mentioned his party. It made him think of those ten minutes in the garage with her. And he didn't want to think about that, not now, not ever.

"Want some?" She held her bottle of iced tea out to him. Michael shook his head. Darcy had just come from the kitchen and was crossing the room holding two cans of soda. She handed him one without acknowledging Amy's presence. Amy stood up, saying she was on her way upstairs to use the bathroom. Darcy sat down in Amy's place without looking at her. It was as if she'd never been there at all.

For the rest of the night Michael went through the motions. He danced dutifully when Darcy suggested it. He accepted the food and drinks she brought him, even though he did not want them. He managed to carry on a conversation with some of his friends, although later he would not remember what they had talked about. He even had the obligatory can of beer out back with a few of the other track stars. By ten most of the kids at the party were drinking beer. Michael knew Darcy hated it when he drank, so he usually didn't.

Steven's parents were upstairs. They had promised not to interfere with his party unless there was trouble. They had no idea that one of the seniors had gotten his older brother to supply the party with a couple of cases of Coors.

By midnight Michael's head was throbbing. He wanted nothing more than to go home to bed. Then, just as Darcy was maneuvering him through the crowd for another dance, he felt a hand clamp down on his shoulder. Joe Sadowski belched his beer-soaked breath in his face. "Hey, man. Haven't seen you all night."

Michael could see that Joe was drunk. His friend could barely stand up. His eyes were a watery pink. He leaned on Michael for support. "The word's out. Your party dropped to second place two cases of Coors ago. Sorry, man." Joe patted him on the back, pretending to be sympathetic.

Darcy looked grim. Michael knew she disliked Joe. She would be even less patient with a drunken Joe. "I'll just take him outside in the fresh air," he told her. "I'll be right back."

Darcy rolled her eyes toward the ceiling, then nodded. She would be out in the kitchen talking with Suzanne, she told him. Suzanne and her boyfriend had broken up only an hour ago.

Michael steered Joe out the back door onto the patio and sat him in a lounge chair. "Man, you're really gassed," he said.

Joe grinned up at him. "That's what parties are for, man. Get with the program." He narrowed his eyes. "You ain't gonna preach to me, I hope?" He shook his head and snorted. "Nah, you wouldn't dare."

Michael didn't have to ask what he meant. His body tensed. He glanced over his shoulder to see if anyone had overheard. He began to worry that Joe might say something to someone—the wrong someone—while he was in this condition, something they'd both regret.

"Come on, I'll take you home," he said.

"Can't go home," Joe slurred. "My folks'll kill me."

Michael considered this for a minute. He didn't want to leave Joe there on the lounge chair. "We have a couple of old sleeping bags in my garage. You can spend the night there," he told him. He thought of calling Joe's folks to let them know Joe would be staying at his house, but then thought better of it. What if they said no? Or worse, asked to speak to Joe?

No, he would have to do this without telling anyone. He only hoped he could get Joe into the garage without too much noise. Michael didn't need his parents calling the police. But as it turned out, the police would have been preoccupied anyway, because at that very moment two officers were standing on Steven Chang's front stoop.

Darcy came bounding through the back door and grabbed Michael's arm. "We'd better get out of here. The cops are out front." For one terrifying moment Michael believed they had come for him. He stared down at Darcy in horror.

"The neighbors are complaining about the noise," she said. "But if the police find out kids have been drinking . . ."

"Help me get him out of here," Michael said.

"What?" Darcy looked down at Joe as if he were a pile of squirming snakes. Her upper lip curled in undisguised revulsion.

Michael knew that if the cops spotted them getting into his car, they'd probably ask to see his license. Especially if they thought he'd been drinking. And walking beside Joe was like holding up a neon sign that screamed GO AHEAD, BUST ME. But he didn't dare leave his friend behind.

"We can't leave him here for the cops to find," Michael said, lifting one of Joe's arms. "Take his other arm."

Together he and Darcy got Joe to his unstable feet and began steering him across the yard, just as another police car rounded the corner.

5

Joe was already gone when Michael checked the garage the next morning. A tangled sleeping bag lay in a heap where he'd spent the night.

Fortunately the police hadn't noticed the three of them leaving the party the night before. He and Darcy had managed to get Joe to the car without further incident, except for a brief detour into the Delaneys' front yard, where Joe vomited into the hydrangea bushes. For a moment Michael had thought Darcy was going to be sick, too. Her face had turned a waxy white in the moonlight. But when he drove her home after helping Joe settle in, all she said was, "Have you ever thought about getting yourself a new best friend?"

Michael neatly rolled up the sleeping bag, put it back on the shelf with the other camping equipment, and stepped outside. Dark clouds hinted at approaching thunderstorms. No one would be at the pool today, although Michael knew he would still be expected to be there. He would spend the day doing indoor jobs for Simon Goldfarb, probably painting over graffiti. Not that he minded this kind of weather. It had been an unusually dry summer so far, and they needed the rain.

A loud clap of thunder echoed in the distance. Michael

headed back to the house. But as he put his hand on the screen door he heard his parents' voices coming from the kitchen. They were talking about the Ward case.

Michael's hand rested for a moment on the doorknob; then he let it drop to his side. He would skip breakfast this morning. Instead he headed straight for the community pool.

He had been right about painting over graffiti. He and the two other male lifeguards spent the day rolling coats of thick white paint over the men's locker room walls, while the three female lifeguards painted the women's locker room.

All that morning he was haunted by the thought of trying to eat another meal with his family while they speculated about Charlie Ward's killer. So during his lunch break Michael called home, knowing full well he'd get the answering machine, and told his mother not to expect him for dinner. Then, because he realized he needed a reason, he added that he was spending the night at Joe's. But even as he said this, he knew that Joe Sadowski's was the last place he would go. Because, like it or not, his best friend had become a part of what Michael so desperately wanted to forget.

It had stopped raining by the time he finished work, although a steamy mist hung over everything, blocking out the sun. Michael walked to the library, planning to read the most recent newspapers. He had forgotten it was Friday night. The library closed at five. For a long time he sat on the front steps, wondering where to go next.

Finally he bought a Coke and a salami-and-tomato on pumpernickel at the Corner Deli, and ate at one of the public picnic tables near the community pool. When he looked at his watch again, it was only six.

For a while he walked around town. Then he wandered down two more blocks, until he came to the end of Main Street, and turned left. He headed up the hill, passing several old Victorian homes, then entered a side street. That was when he suddenly realized where he'd been going all along. For there, across the street from him, stood a large blue-gray house with elegant white scrollwork. Jenna Ward's house. He realized then that it hadn't been just idle curiosity that had prompted him to look up her address in the phone book three nights ago. He had needed to come here.

Michael sat down on the curb. Even through the heavy haze, he could see the neatly manicured lawn and the rows of thorny bushes drooping under the burden of fat wet roses. Everything looked still and misty, as if it had been stopped in time. There was something ghostlike about it.

He shivered, feeling the damp curb through his cutoffs. Part of his backside rested on wet grass. But he could not bring himself to leave, even though he had no idea why he had come.

He wondered if the family belonged to the community pool, then decided they didn't. If they did, he would have recognized Jenna; he was sure of it. Maybe they had their own pool. Judging from the house and the part of town they lived in, it seemed a reasonable assumption. Michael decided they probably spent at least part of their summers on Martha's Vineyard, or Nantucket, or someplace like that.

When he stood up to keep his pants from getting any wetter, he noticed he was only a few yards from the front of a church. If he sat on the stairs, his presence would seem less obvious to anyone in the neighborhood who might notice. So he positioned himself on the top step, resting his back against the heavy oak doors. And there he kept his vigil until the street-lights blinked on.

The moon was almost full that night, but Michael did not notice until he came to an unlit road. The blue-white glow spilled down through the leaves, and the trees cast their inky shadows across the road. It was a quiet street, one he had never been on before. He kept walking, because he had already been all over town, and because there was nothing else to do and nowhere to go.

When he reached the end of the road, he saw, in the moonlight, a Cape Cod house, small and neat and white. A name plaque dangled from a post by the split-rail fence. The letters burned into his tired eyes, forming the name *Ruggerio*. He wondered if this could possibly be Amy's home.

Somehow he had never pictured Amy living in a house, although he didn't know why that should be. But as it turned out, this *was* her house, because suddenly there was Amy, standing in front of him in her white shorts and pink tank top, as if she'd been expecting him all along. She smiled a shy hello; then, gently taking his arm, she led him inside. Michael couldn't tell if she was surprised that he'd suddenly shown up at her house or not. He decided not to question any of what was happening. His instincts told him it was better that way.

Everything inside was neat and clean, but the furniture seemed too big for such a small house. Old and overstuffed, it seemed to push up against the walls, as if trying to burst through them. Amy pointed him in the direction of a large, bulky couch. As Michael sat down he noticed a pale brown stain on the front of his T-shirt. He realized he must have spilled some of his Coke earlier but hadn't been aware of it. He wished he could hide the stain somehow. He thought about turning his shirt around when she left the room. For some reason it seemed important not to let Amy think he'd shown up at her house looking like a slob.

"Want something to eat?" she said.

Michael nodded, although he really wasn't hungry. He still could not understand how he had come to be at Amy's. Had he seen her address somewhere? He'd heard about things like that. How the brain stored away little bits and pieces of seemingly useless information, which suddenly popped up at the most unexpected times.

Amy left the room. When she came back, she was carrying a tray with a pitcher of iced tea, two glasses filled with ice, and a half-empty box of Fig Newtons. She set the tray on the coffee table in front of the couch where Michael was already settling in, letting himself sink comfortably into the soft cushions. By then he had forgotten all about turning his shirt around.

"Are you here alone?" he asked, glad to discover that his voice sounded relatively normal.

Amy poured a glass of iced tea and handed it to him. "Pappy's upstairs sleeping."

"Your dad?" Michael took the glass from her. The icy wetness cooled his sweating palms.

"My grandfather."

"He lives here with you?"

A soft smile curved the corners of her full mouth. "I live here with him," she corrected. "Gram died a little over a year ago."

Michael did not ask about her parents. It was enough for the moment to know she had a grandfather. Enough to know that she wasn't totally alone in the world, although he wasn't sure why that should matter to him.

"We can watch a movie if you want," she said, pointing to the VCR next to the TV.

He cleared his throat. "What kind of movies do you have?"

Amy seemed to hesitate. "Mostly romantic stuff," she said, barely whispering. Her face flushed a delicate pink, which both surprised and touched him. He realized then, for the first time that evening, that she wasn't wearing makeup. Her face looked scrubbed and polished. She bit into a Fig Newton, looking thoughtful. "Or we could play a game. I have Scrabble."

Michael said Scrabble was fine, although he didn't feel much like playing. But Amy seemed pleased. And it would keep his mind off other things.

They set up the board on the coffee table, pulling cushions from the couch onto the floor. Then they settled themselves on the cushions and, like an old married couple, played Scrabble and ate Fig Newtons until, exhausted, they fell asleep on the floor.

When the first rays of light began to filter through the sheer white curtains, Amy rose and went about turning off the lights. Michael waited by the front door.

"I hope we didn't disturb your grandfather."

Amy grinned. "Couldn't you hear him snoring?"

"Well, yeah, but . . ."

"He sleeps like a log." She looked down at her bare feet. The sunlight caught the top of her head, turning her dark brown hair a rich auburn. Michael felt an overwhelming desire to touch that spot on her head. "I'm glad you came over," she said simply.

Without looking, Michael reached for the doorknob. "I

didn't mean to stay so long," he told her. But they both knew he had.

"It's okay. Nobody'll find out."

Something inside him cringed. In that single moment he realized that Amy was perfectly aware of what the other kids thought of her, although he was beginning to wonder just how true those stories were. And he also knew, beyond a doubt, that she would keep his visit a secret.

Michael turned and stepped outside into the damp morning air. He knew that if he stayed another minute, he would kiss her goodbye.

Amy waved to him, watching as he walked out to the road, then slowly closed the door. He was alone again, only this time the aloneness had a sharper edge to it.

He looked back at the small house he'd just come from. Sunlight poured down the front of it like fresh cream. Where was he to go from here? It seemed as though each new day became more complicated, more exhausting. He spent all his waking hours trying to get away from someone: from Darcy, from Joe, from his parents, and maybe even from Amy, because he realized he probably wouldn't be coming to her house again.

The rest of the summer still loomed ahead of him like some vast desert he had to cross. Then would come September and school. He wondered how much longer he could keep avoiding people, lying to them. How much longer could he keep dodging the inevitable?

jenna

f or two days after her father's death, hundreds of enormous dragonflies blanketed Jenna's front yard. No one knew where they came from or why they darted about haphazardly, barely two feet above the ground, with their iridescent wings, their blue-green bodies, shimmering in the sunlight. Like miniature aircraft with defective gyroscopes, they shot out in all directions, coming within a fraction of an inch of colliding with each other.

Neighbors who never went for walks and had little interest in physical fitness suddenly took leisurely strolls along the sidewalk, slowing their pace to a virtual standstill as they approached the Ward house. They did not know what to make of the strange sight. So they simply shook their heads and called it a sign—but of what, they had no idea.

All this time Jenna hardly noticed the dragonflies or the curious neighbors. At night she sometimes slept curled on the wicker chaise longue on the front porch because the air-conditioning in the house numbed the tips of her fingers and toes. On those nights cicadas hummed their own deep, mysterious song while a mournful owl in a nearby oak tree wailed the chorus. And in the morning the pillow would be wet with tears Jenna had cried in her sleep.

Something else came with the night: a disturbing dream. A dream choked with thick, twisted tree trunks, big enough to hide a bear, and tangled vines that coiled around her body, pulling her deeper and deeper into a mist-clouded forest. Through the vapor Jenna could make out the bare bone-white branches of a giant tree. And as the vines pulled at her ankles she tugged against them with all her strength. She would not go to this place. Nothing, not all the vines on the face of the earth, could make her go there.

In daylight the dream made no sense. Whenever Jenna thought about the tree, it didn't seem frightening at all. She knew this place, this old sycamore. Everybody called it the Ghost Tree. It was a place steeped in mystery and folklore. Jenna had spent happy hours there as a child. She would have laughed at her fears had the dream lasted only one night. But she had dreamt it three nights in a row. Each time she had to fight the vines even harder, and each morning she awoke exhausted.

❖

In the days following her father's death Jenna's house was never empty. Family came, neighbors came, her mother's co-workers, Jenna's classmates, her father's friends; they filled every room. They brought cakes and covered dishes. They shared their stories, their memories of Charlie Ward. And when Jenna could take no more, she locked herself in her room. No one thought it the least bit odd—although they might not have understood the pleasure she got each time she walked into her room.

Over the past few days she had rearranged everything.

Now every object on her dresser was carefully aligned. The bedspread was smooth and taut, not a single wrinkle. Every piece of clothing in her closet was neatly lined up by color, and every shoe was snuggled beside its mate in tidy rows.

Each time she left her room, she inspected every inch to make sure nothing was out of place. And when she returned, the comfort she felt in finding such order was so intense, she wanted to cry. Each and every object was always just as she'd left it. Nothing had changed.

Perhaps the people downstairs might have thought this strange if they had seen her room only a few days earlier: chaotic heaps of discarded dirty clothes, crusty plates, glasses gummy with dried soda, papers and open books tossed haphazardly in corners. But that room had belonged to another Jenna.

They might have thought it unusual, too, that she spent many of those private hours, after she'd retreated to her well-ordered sanctuary, working on math problems. But Jenna couldn't have cared less what they thought. Math was her passion.

She could never make those people downstairs understand that she found these equations more comforting than their sympathetic words and hugs. Solving math problems cleared her mind; it left no room for anything else. Equations produced only one correct answer. You either got it right or you didn't. There was no middle ground. No murky gray area to confuse you.

On the morning of the funeral, her mother stood in Jenna's doorway staring at her daughter's attire. Her well-shaped eyebrows slid into a frown.

"What?" Jenna smoothed her long skirt, then spread her hands palms up. She looked down at her heavy lace-up boots. It had rained all the previous day and most of the night. The grass at the cemetery would be wet, the ground muddy. The boots were a practical decision. Her mother, the queen of practicality, should have been able to see that. Jenna braced herself for an argument.

But Meredith Ward, much to Jenna's surprise, simply shrugged and began absently brushing at a wrinkle in her skirt. She said nothing. Her own outfit was perfectly coordinated. Jenna noticed she wore high-heeled black patent leather shoes. The heels were sure to sink into the soft mud, throwing her mother off balance. The image of her mother suddenly tipping over in front of all those people made Jenna smile, while at the same time a wave of shame for even thinking such a thing on the day of her father's funeral washed over her, dampening her amusement.

Jenna hiked up her skirt, put her foot on the bedspread, and double-knotted the shoelace, trying to ignore her mother.

Meredith Ward hovered in the doorway for another minute, although Jenna was no longer sure why. Then, much to her relief, her mother turned and headed downstairs.

The rest of the morning was a blur. People she had never met, coworkers from her father's office, took her hand and whispered their muted words of sympathy. Close friends and family swarmed about her in the hot, sticky air until she thought she might suffocate. Overhead the dark clouds rumbled and threatened, but the rain never came. And when it was time to leave, Jenna stared down at the casket in front of her and wondered again, for the thousandth time, what she was supposed to be feeling.

On the hot July evenings that followed, while bees hovered lazily over the borders of pink impatiens, Jenna lay in the hammock by the pool waiting for her father to come home from work. She would find herself doing this and then realize that it was not going to happen.

Sometimes, when she opened her eyes slowly, the shadows from the trees in the woods behind her house played tricks and made her believe she actually saw him. But on this particular night, just as the fireflies began to appear, the shadow that moved toward her from the wooded path turned out to be Andrea Sloan, her best friend.

Andrea lived in the house behind Jenna's on the next street over. Their houses, like all of the homes on the block, were separated by a thick wooded area that spanned about fifty yards. Over the years the two girls had worn a footpath between their two backyards.

Andrea pulled an aluminum chair over to where Jenna lay in the hammock and sat down. She put her hand on the edge of the hammock and began to rock it back and forth as if she were rocking a cradle. "Come to the pool with me tomorrow. I can get you a guest badge."

Jenna folded her arms behind her head and stared up at the stars. "Why? We can swim here."

"Yeah, but everybody else will be at the community pool."

Jenna looked over at her friend. Andrea had let go of the side of the hammock and was tugging nervously at a tight ringlet of short dark hair.

"I'd feel weird," Jenna told her.

"Why?"

"Well, everybody at the funeral . . . you know . . . was being so . . . nice. It gave me the creeps."

"Yeah? So? You don't want them to feel bad about what happened to your dad?" Andrea looked confused.

Jenna sighed. "It's not that. I just hate the idea of people feeling sorry for me."

Andrea sat back and plunked her bare feet unceremoniously on Jenna's stomach, using it for a footrest. "I don't feel sorry for you," she said.

"You don't?"

"No. I think it really stinks, what happened to your dad. But I don't feel sorry for you." She made a face. "That would be like pity or something. I don't do pity."

Jenna laughed. "At least not very well, anyway."

Andrea lowered her feet back to the ground. "Besides, Jason's coming home tonight, isn't he? So he'll probably be there."

Jenna had had a crush on Jason Friedman since the seventh grade. Then finally, in April, they had started going out. She had never been happier. Now she realized with amazement that she hadn't even thought about him these past weeks.

Jason and his family always spent part of July camping in Maine. It occurred to her that Jason probably didn't even know about her dad. How could he? His family had left before it had happened. And since his father always elected to go camping in remote places that had no phones or plumbing, insisting his family could live without television and newspapers for a few weeks, the chances of their having heard about the accident were practically nil.

"Come on," Andrea coaxed, "it'll be fun."

Jenna looked down at her bare feet and wiggled her toes. "I don't know. Maybe some other time."

"Some other time? That's it?" Andrea reached over and pinched Jenna on the forearm.

Jenna jumped. "Hey."

"I just wanted to make sure you were still alive."

"Well, I am," Jenna snapped, "so you can keep your hands to yourself."

Andrea slapped her palms on her thighs and took a deep breath to show her disgust. "I just thought you'd want to get out of the house. Face it, Jen, you haven't been anywhere in weeks. You can't hang out in your house forever."

A cool breeze skimmed over Jenna's bare arms and legs. She wanted to tell Andrea that yes, she could hang out in her house forever. And she might have said just that if Andrea hadn't gripped the side of the hammock again and begun tugging it back and forth. Jenna grabbed the sides and held on.

"Are you listening to me?" Andrea shouted. "I mean, Jen, there have been parties practically every night around here. How are you going to meet any seniors if you don't go to parties?"

Jenna didn't respond. She doubted she'd ever want to go to another party for as long as she lived. At parties she would have to pretend that everything was fine, as if her father's death had been just some brief interruption in her life and now everything was back to normal. It would be too painful.

Andrea locked her arms across her chest. "I'm not going to give up until you say you'll go with me to the pool. I'll come over here every day and drive you crazy until you say yes," she said, thrusting her chin forward.

Jenna had to laugh. She knew how stubborn Andrea could be. She'd nag her until she gave in. Jenna also understood that her friend was only trying to help. "Okay," she said finally. "I'll go. Happy now?"

"Ecstatic," Andrea said, standing up. And she did look pleased, as if she had completed some secret mission. "I'll come over about ten, okay?"

"Right. Ten." Jenna watched her friend cross the yard. Then she lay back, closed her eyes, and imagined Jason had been the one to wander into the yard that evening instead of Andrea.

When Jenna went inside a few minutes later, she headed straight for the refrigerator. Neither she nor her mother had bothered much with regular meals, eating only when they thought of it, which wasn't often. Jenna hadn't eaten anything since breakfast.

She studied the casserole dishes and the endless stacks of Tupperware filled with soups and salads. Edible condolences from friends and neighbors. Even now, people were still stopping by unexpectedly to leave freshly baked blueberry muffins or a tortellini salad. Jenna wondered if it would ever end.

Overwhelmed by the profusion of colored plastic, she reached for the most convenient container, which happened to be filled with potato salad that had gone bad. She gagged, and stuffed the salad back into the refrigerator. Finally, without giving it much thought, she slapped together a peanut butter sandwich, then tossed the gummy knife into a sink full of unwashed dishes.

The house was silent except for the distant hum of the refrigerator as she wandered from room to room, idly chewing the sandwich. Dozens of wilting flower arrangements, sent by well-meaning friends—in spite of the family's request that the money be donated to charity instead—still sat on tables in the living room and dining room. The water in their containers had become stagnant. The two rooms smelled sour. Jenna held her nose as she walked through.

When she reached the family room, she found her mother asleep on the couch. A half-eaten slice of whole wheat toast, thinly coated with grape jelly, sat on a plate on the floor. A tiny blob of jelly stained the front of her mother's light blue T-shirt. On the floor in front of the couch lay a flower-print comforter.

Jenna shivered, stuffed the last bite of her sandwich into her mouth, and rubbed her upper arms. The room was ice-cold. The air-conditioning was on full blast, as usual.

She lifted the comforter from the floor and gently laid it over her mother.

Meredith Ward blinked and, with eyes only half open, said, "Jen?"

"Yeah?"

Her mother nuzzled her cheek against one of the throw pillows. "Did you have dinner yet?"

Jenna wiped the peanut butter from her fingers onto her shorts. "Yeah."

"Good." Her mother's eyes closed again.

Jenna stood for a while, her arms dangling limply at her sides, watching her mother. During the past few weeks they had been unusually careful with each other. There had been no arguments, no scenes, yet Jenna felt an overwhelming sense of loneliness. She hesitated for a moment, then said, "Mom?"

"Hmmm?"

"Have you ever wondered why? I mean, why us? Why Daddy?" She had been plagued by these questions but hadn't dared to ask them out loud.

Her mother was awake now. She sat up, shoving the comforter into a ball at the end of the couch, then stared at it for a few minutes. Jenna saw that the rims of her eyes were swollen and red. She envied her mother her tears.

Finally her mother said, "I don't have an answer for that, Jen."

"Is it something we did? I mean, I know this sounds really childish, but I can't help feeling like we're being punished."

Meredith reached for Jenna's hand and pulled her down beside her on the couch. "I know I'm *supposed* to say something reasonable, like 'There aren't any simple answers to these things. They just happen. It's not because of anything we did.'" She began to pick at the dried jelly on her T-shirt. Her eyes grew moist. "I never realized before how ridiculously simplistic those words sound." She rubbed her eyes. "I'm sorry. I'm not being very helpful, am I?"

"It's okay, Mom. It'd be worse if you started spouting all those hollow clichés just to make me feel better."

Her mother took a deep breath. "What keeps going through my mind is, I did everything I was supposed to, and this is how it turns out! I feel . . . I don't know . . . cheated, somehow."

Jenna shook her head. "I don't understand. What do you mean, everything you were supposed to do?"

Meredith continued to scrape at the stubborn jelly stain. Jenna saw that her mother had been picking at the skin around her cuticles. Her fingers looked raw.

"I'm not sure, really. I suppose I thought all I had to do was play by the rules. If I worked hard, if I was a good wife and mother, if I was good at my job, kept a neat house . . ." Her voice trailed off. She pulled a soggy tissue from her pocket and blew her nose. "I guess what I thought was, if I did all those things, we'd all live to a ripe old age." She snorted a little laugh and looked over at Jenna. Her mouth was twisted in an awkward half smile.

Jenna tried to think of something to say, but no words would come.

Her mother leaned over and brushed a strand of Jenna's hair behind her ear. "Marge Evans from work told me that I shouldn't think of myself as a victim. She says what happened to us is part of life."

"Yeah, the rotten part."

Meredith squeezed her eyes shut and pressed her hand hard against her mouth. After a few minutes she said, "I'm so sorry, Jen. I wish you hadn't seen me like this. I'm supposed to be the strong one. I should be comforting you. And here I am— Oh, God, I must sound so angry. But I can't help it. I keep thinking I failed him in some way, you know? That there was something I could have—*should have*—done. And if I'd only done it, he'd still be here."

Jenna felt as if her entire body had been weighted down with rocks. She wasn't even sure she'd be able to get up off the couch when the time came. "There's nothing you could have done, Mom."

Her mother reached for the comforter at the end of the couch and stretched it across both of them. She pulled the edge up beneath her chin and lowered her face into the soft folds.

Jenna let her head flop against the back of the couch and closed her eyes. "I still keep expecting him to come home."

Her mother sighed softly. "Me too," she said.

Jenna entered her bedroom an hour later without turning on the light. She had been doing this ever since the evening she'd noticed the boy sitting on the front steps of the church across the street. The first time she saw him from her bedroom window had been two days after her father's death. He had been sitting on the top step, leaning back against the church doors. Jenna thought he looked familiar. But at the time she hadn't paid much attention. Two evenings later he was there again.

At first she hadn't been sure it was the same person. The second time she saw him, the boy had his arms wrapped around his legs, which were drawn up to his chest, and his forehead pressed against his knees. But when he finally stretched his legs forward, letting his head fall back against the door, the setting sun spilled over his face, and she knew for certain it was the same boy. She thought she recognized him from school, although she didn't know his name. She had wondered what he was doing waiting outside the church, then decided he was probably meeting someone.

But on the evenings when he showed up—and she had counted ten so far—Jenna never saw anyone else. And when she looked out her window after dark, he would always be gone. So she really had no way of knowing if the person he was waiting for had come or not.

Tonight the streetlight cast leafy shadows on the empty stone steps of the church. If the boy had been there earlier, he had already left. Still, she had to wonder why he came.

7

The next morning Jenna sat on the deck eating an English muffin, waiting for Andrea to show up. The branches of two giant sugar maples formed a canopy overhead. They waved gently in the breeze. It was an unusually clear and cool morning for late July.

Gazing up at the branches, Jenna was suddenly reminded of her dream about the Ghost Tree. The same dream that had continued to haunt her night after night since her father's death. She could feel the pull of the forest, the helplessness of her own body as it was dragged along by the tangled mass of vines. She hated the sensation of being out of control. It terrified her.

It was better not to think about the dream. Instead she took another bite of her muffin and thought of Jason Friedman.

And the first thing she did, when she arrived at the pool a half hour later, was look for him. But he was nowhere in sight.

"Don't worry, he'll be here," Andrea whispered as several of their friends crowded around them. Jenna hugged those she hadn't seen since the funeral, glad to see them. She felt, at least for the moment, as if nothing had changed. Although she didn't try to kid herself.

Then she unfolded her beach towel and sat down. She had just begun to smear suntan lotion on her arms when she saw Jason coming toward her. He seemed to have gotten taller since she'd last seen him, and a little thinner. But he still had the same impish face, though his usual grin was absent at the moment. He sat down on the grass next to her and put his arm around her shoulder, then let it drop. The half hug was awkward, as if he wasn't sure it was the right thing to do.

"I'm really sorry about what happened to your dad," he said. "I just found out this morning. We didn't get home till late last night. I called your house a little while ago, but nobody answered. I guess you'd already left."

Jenna only nodded. She couldn't seem to speak.

"Jeez, I feel rotten." He reached for her hand. "I should have been here with you."

Something odd was happening. Her heart was racing furiously, and not in the way it used to when she was near Jason. This was entirely different. The pounding was so intense it filled her ears and blocked out all other sounds.

When she still didn't say anything, Jason put his hand on her shoulder, tilting his head so that he could look directly into her face. "I feel like I've really let you down. I'm sorry."

Jenna shook her head, trying to reassure him. "It's okay. You couldn't have known." She found herself struggling to take a breath.

"It must be tough."

"It is." The words poured out on a whispered rush of trapped air. Jenna gasped, then took a deep breath.

Andrea, who had been listening to every word, leaned forward and tapped her arm. "Are you okay?"

"It's the heat," Jenna said. She stood up and nodded

toward the water. "I'm going in." Out of the corner of her eye she saw Andrea and Jason exchange concerned looks.

She sat down on the edge of the pool and let her feet dangle in the cool water, hoping neither Andrea nor Jason would follow her. She closed her eyes and took deep swallows of air. With each breath, the smell of chlorine stung her nose.

When she opened her eyes, she thought she caught one of the lifeguards on the other side of the pool watching her, although it was difficult to tell since he was wearing sunglasses. Something about him seemed familiar.

"You sure you're okay?" Jenna felt a hand on her shoulder as Andrea sat down beside her.

"I'm sure. It's the heat, that's all." Jenna was still studying the lifeguard.

"He's cute, isn't he?" Andrea said.

"Who?"

"The lifeguard you're staring at."

"I wasn't staring at him."

"Well, I wouldn't blame you if you were."

Jenna turned to her friend. Andrea was kicking at the water with her feet and watching the lifeguard. She hadn't shown any interest in anyone since Tony Coletti had broken up with her four months ago, and Jenna had begun to think her friend had sworn off boys permanently. It was good to see Andrea interested in someone again.

"Who is he, do you know?"

"His name is Michael MacKenzie. He's going to be a senior. And he's a jock . . . a big track star at school."

"He sounds a little too good to be true. What's the catch?"

Andrea slid into the pool and rested her arms on the edge. "Well, there is this one tiny problem."

"Which is?"

"He's got a girlfriend." She tilted her head in the direction of a group of kids playing cards beneath a nearby tree. "She's the one with the long red hair. Her name's Darcy Kelly."

"You call that a tiny problem?"

Andrea pursed her lips. "Okay, big problem."

Jenna squinted to get a better look at Michael MacKenzie. His lips and nose were covered with white ointment, and the metallic glint of his sunglasses completely hid his eyes. He probably hadn't been watching her at all before, she thought. She'd only imagined it. He was just doing his job, keeping a sharp eye on all the swimmers. Still, there was something about him . . .

When she got home that afternoon, Jenna made her daily call to Chief Zelenski. She'd been doing this for two weeks now, sometimes calling twice a day, hoping for information. But this time he wasn't in when she called.

Disappointed, she left a message, then headed up to her room to work on math problems. She had just started on the first equation when Jason called.

"Can I see you tonight?" he asked.

Jenna, silent, held the cordless phone a few inches away from her face and stared at it. Something was terribly wrong. Her hand was shaking so badly that the phone had been tapping the side of her head.

"Jen?"

She put the phone as close to her ear as she dared. Her heart was racing so fast she couldn't catch her breath. It was happening again. Just as it had at the pool earlier. Only this was worse.

"What?" She barely managed to get the word out.

"Uh, is this a bad time? I mean, do you want me to call back later?"

She tried to remember what her drama teacher at school had taught her about controlling stage fright. Because that was what this felt like, only ten times more severe. And she couldn't for the life of her imagine what was causing it. *Breathe*, she told herself. *Long, deep breaths. Focus.*

"Hey! You still there?" Jason was beginning to sound alarmed.

"Yes. Sorry." *Breathe, Jen. Breathe.* "Tonight?"

"Is that okay? I mean, that's all I thought about the whole time I was in Maine. You know? Seeing you."

Jenna walked over to the window, concentrating on her breathing the entire time. Outside, the late-afternoon sun bathed the front of the church across the street in a soft glow. That was when she saw the boy mounting the steps of the church and taking his place in front of the door. This was the earliest she had ever seen him there. Then, for the first time, she realized he was staring over at her house. A slight shiver ran along her spine.

"I wanted to ask you at the pool," Jason was saying, "but we didn't get much of a chance to be alone."

"Tonight's fine," she told him, because she could think of no reason not to see him.

"Seven? Maybe we can catch a movie at the mall."

She shifted the phone to her other hand and wiped her sweaty palm on her shorts. All the while she continued to focus on her breathing. "Okay . . . well, then . . . see you."

Relieved to have the awkward conversation over, Jenna hung up the phone. Then she turned her attention back to the boy across the street. She thought he looked like the lifeguard from the pool, but she couldn't be absolutely sure.

The boy was no longer staring at her house. He had curled himself into the same position she had seen him in many times. And each time he did, she was reminded of the hermit crabs, curling into their scavenged shells, that she sometimes found along the Nantucket beach, near the Wards' summer rental.

She could not have said why, but something deep inside her seemed to sense his pain. That was why she stood, her forehead pressed against the window screen, watching over the boy until she heard her mother's car in the driveway.

meredith Ward came through the back door balancing two bags of groceries and her briefcase. Without a word, Jenna grabbed one of the bags and set it on the counter.

Her mother began putting away the groceries, all the while grumbling about one of her clients.

"That Porter woman at Fennel is going to drive me into an early grave," she announced, slamming two cans of soup onto one of the cabinet shelves. Then, as if she suddenly realized her unfortunate choice of words, she rested her palms on the kitchen counter and took a deep breath. "Sorry. Bad day."

Jenna knew the Fennel department store chain was one of her mother's biggest accounts. "Want me to fix dinner?" she asked. Usually she wasn't this accommodating. But her mother looked thoroughly exhausted. Besides, she wanted to get dinner over with as soon as possible so that she'd have enough time to take a shower before Jason showed up.

"Oh, would you?" Her mother seemed grateful. "I'd love to take a few laps in the pool and cool off." Then she laughed. "I guess you can tell I need cooling off."

Her mother went upstairs and returned wearing her bathing suit and carrying a towel. "Make it something light, okay?" she said. "I'm not really all that hungry."

From the kitchen window, Jenna watched as her mother stepped onto the diving board. Meredith Ward was an excellent swimmer, and probably the most graceful diver Jenna had ever seen. She barely made a splash when she hit the water.

After a few minutes Jenna turned her attention to dinner. What could she make that was light? She began to rummage through the refrigerator. She finally decided on a simple salad and some yogurt with fruit and granola mixed in.

She was adding fresh strawberries to the yogurt when her mother, towel wrapped around her wet hair, came into the kitchen. "I needed that," she said. "There is absolutely nothing like a few laps across the pool to work out a little tension." She lifted her shoulders up to her ears a few times, then tipped her head first to the right, then to the left, stretching her muscles.

Her mother glanced at the table. "That salad looks terrific." She reached into the cupboard for two glasses. "I'll pour us some iced tea."

Jenna finished stirring the strawberries into the yogurt. When she turned to set the bowl on the table, she realized her mother was still standing in front of the refrigerator. The glasses sat empty on the counter.

"Mom?"

Meredith Ward was staring at something on the refrigerator door. She lifted her hand as if it were made of concrete and pressed it against a sheet of paper.

Jenna looked over her mother's shoulder. The door was plastered with photos, dentist and doctor appointment cards, lists, cartoons, and various clutter all held in place by an assortment of magnets. She saw that her mother's hand was resting on a sheet of lined notepaper. Jenna recognized her father's "Honey Do" list.

"Who crossed this off?" Her mother's voice was barely audible.

"Crossed what off?" But Jenna knew she was talking about the first item on the list: PATCH LEAK IN ROOF. She wanted to snatch the paper from the door and tear it into a thousand pieces.

A deep, gut-wrenching moan came from her mother. It was so sudden and so startling that Jenna could only close her eyes and press her lips tightly together. And for one agonizing moment the cry felt as if it were coming from her own body.

When she opened her eyes, she saw her mother standing with her forehead against the refrigerator door, her hand still on the list, shaking with convulsive sobs. Jenna put her arms around her and led her to a chair.

Then, because she needed to be doing something, she poured two glasses of iced tea and set one in front of her mother along with a box of Kleenex.

Meredith had stopped crying. She grabbed a handful of tissues and blew her nose. "It's strange, isn't it? That list has been there for weeks. I've been in and out of the refrigerator a hundred times since that day, but I never even noticed. Then, suddenly, there it is, staring me right in the face."

Jenna wished she had thrown the list away that same morning she had crossed off the first chore. "I'll clean off the fridge for you, okay? There's a lot of old junk stuck up there."

"Sometimes these things just catch me off guard." Her mother wiped her eyes with the wad of tissues. "The other day I was rummaging in the medicine cabinet for the Visine—I hate going around with my eyes all red—and there was this stuff that was supposed to make his hair grow . . . he was so worried about losing his hair. I just stood there holding that bottle, and suddenly I burst into tears."

Jenna shifted uneasily in her chair.

"I guess that phone call this afternoon set me off," her mother said.

"What phone call?"

Her mother didn't answer. Instead she reached for another handful of tissues. Then she picked up her glass of iced tea, lifted it in the direction of the sliding glass doors that led to the deck, and said, "Let's go outside for a while, okay? We need to talk."

Jenna glanced at the clock. It was only five-thirty. There would still be enough time to eat and take a shower before Jason came. But something in the way her mother had said "We need to talk" had put her on guard. In the days before her father's death, that usually meant Jenna was in some kind of trouble.

Still, her instincts told her this was far more serious. So she followed her mother onto the deck and sat across from her. Her suspicions were confirmed when her mother leaned forward, gently rested her hand on Jenna's arm, and said that Chief Zelenski had called her at work that afternoon.

every muscle in Jenna's body felt cemented in place. She did not dare move or breathe. Had the police found her father's killer? For whenever she tried to picture the person behind that lethal trigger, she could only think of him as a murderer. A cold-blooded killer. It did not matter that the shooting had been an accident. It would never matter. "Well, what did he say? Did they find the person who did it?"

Her mother shook her head. "No. But he says the ballistics team traced the path of the bullet to within a four-block area."

Four blocks. Somewhere within a mere four blocks the killer might be sitting in his home. Maybe watching television, or eating dinner. Normal stuff. Jenna noticed her hands had begun to shake, and she set her glass of iced tea on the arm of the chair. "So now what?"

"Well, Dave says the local police have been going door-to-door asking questions. They're trying to find out who has a gun that matches the bullet."

An aborted laugh stuck in Jenna's throat. "You're serious, right? They really think, with all the publicity about the accident, that anybody's going to admit they even own a gun?"

Her mother unwrapped the towel from her head, wiped

her swollen eyes with it, then began to rub her wet hair. "They have records," she said. "Handguns have to be registered. They know who owns what."

"What if it wasn't a handgun?"

Her mother's eyes met hers, and Jenna could almost feel her disappointment. "You mean maybe it was a rifle?"

Jenna shrugged. "Why not?"

"I'm not sure rifles have to be registered." Her mother combed the wet strands of hair with her fingers and stared out at the woods behind the house. "If it was a rifle, then it might be harder for them to track down." Her mother's words came slowly.

"Or what if it's an illegal handgun?" Jenna said. "Not everybody plays by the rules, Mom."

Her mother looked upset. Jenna knew just how she felt. They had been waiting for three weeks for news, hoping that by now the police had found something, anything, to give them both a little peace of mind.

"Well, I guess we'll just have to leave it up to them." Meredith Ward stood up and headed toward the sliding glass door. "In the meantime, let's go enjoy that lovely dinner you made."

"I'm not very hungry," Jenna told her. "You go ahead."

Meredith nodded as if she understood. "I have to admit, I don't have much of an appetite myself."

Jenna couldn't say why, but she had an eerie sense that Chief Zelenski hadn't told them everything. Maybe her mother was willing to leave it all up to the police, but Jenna couldn't bear the thought of just sitting back and doing nothing.

As soon as her mother went inside, Jenna raced down the steps and headed for town. If Chief Zelenski was holding out on them, she wanted to know why. She ran the whole way to the police station, and when she came bursting through the front door, the officer at the desk, an overweight man with a red jowly face, merely stared at her with tired, indifferent eyes. Jenna recognized him as Doug Boyle, the officer all the kids called the Hangman, although she had no idea why.

"I need to see Chief Zelenski," she told him, wiping the sweat from her forehead with her arm.

"You're that Ward kid, right?"

Jenna nodded.

Officer Boyle was eyeing her suspiciously. "Is this an emergency?"

"It's important."

"Yeah, but is it an *emergency*?"

Jenna was growing angrier by the minute. Apparently her reputation for making daily phone calls to the station was well known. "No. But I need to talk to him."

"Well, he just stepped out." Doug Boyle jerked his thumb in the direction of the clock on the wall. "He'll be back in about fifteen minutes."

Jenna looked around, saw a row of brown plastic chairs by the wall near the front door, and said she'd wait.

Boyle shrugged. "Suit yourself. He's gonna be tied up for a while when he gets back. Probably won't be able to see you right away."

If an ax had been handy, Jenna thought, she would have hacked the man's desk into splinters. She had an overwhelming need to smash her fist into something—a window, a door, Boyle's face, something she could damage.

Doug Boyle probably already knew the major suspects in the case. He had information that she, Jenna, had every right to. But she knew he wasn't about to give it out. She forced her body to move toward the chairs, took a seat, and tried to calm herself down. She couldn't let Chief Zelenski see her like this. He would think she was just some irrational teenage girl. And maybe, in that moment, she was. Because for the first time since her father's death, she felt a passionate desire for revenge.

The police chief was no more help than Doug Boyle. But at least he took the time to talk to her when he got back, although all he did was confirm that they were in the process of questioning people from the area the ballistics team had outlined.

"Which is where?" Jenna asked.

"You don't need to know that," he said. The wire-rimmed glasses slid down his nose, just as they had on that first morning.

Jenna shrugged. "It's probably all over town by now, anyway. I'll just ask Mrs. Rico." Annie Rico worked behind the cosmetics counter at her husband's pharmacy and was always delighted to share what she knew, which was just about everything that was going on in town.

Chief Zelenski pulled at his lower lip with his thumb and forefinger. "You're right. Annie Rico probably does know." Then he laughed. "I should talk to her. I bet she knows more about this case than I do."

Jenna was not amused. She left the police station feeling as if nobody really cared, although Dave Zelenski had been very nice about it all, including her steady stream of daily phone calls.

Not surprisingly, Mrs. Rico did know which area the police were investigating. She leaned over the cosmetics counter conspiratorially—so far over, in fact, that Jenna could clearly see the half inch of dark roots at the base of her bright yellow hair—and whispered with her Listermint breath that the cops were bound to nail the killer any day now. Then she told Jenna that the four-block area was on the other side of town, between Maple and Elm streets, west of Main Street.

Jenna felt humiliated at having to ask the town gossip for information she believed should have come from the police, but she was desperate to know, and Mrs. Rico was her only source.

Once she stepped outside the pharmacy, however, Jenna had no idea where to begin. What was she going to do? Go from door to door herself? The police were already doing that. Disappointed, she headed back home, only to find Jason sitting in the living room drinking a Pepsi and talking to her mother.

Jenna's hand went instinctively to her hair, which clung to her sweating face and neck in clumps. She shoved her damp hair behind her ears, mortified. She must have looked a fright. Even worse, she had completely forgotten their date.

"Sorry I'm late," she said, trying to act as if she hadn't really forgotten about him at all. "I had something I needed to do."

Her mother and Jason were staring at her openly.

"No problem," Jason said. "I just got here."

"Give me a minute to change my clothes, okay? I'll be right back." Then, without waiting for a response, she darted upstairs.

On the bus on the way to the mall, Jason said, "Your mom told me what the ballistics team found out. That's good news."

"Yeah, it is." She hadn't felt this awkward around Jason since seventh grade. But at least she wasn't having those weird panicky feelings that she'd had earlier. "How's your science project?" she asked, because she had no idea what else to talk about.

"Okay. Vacation set me back, but I'm coming up to speed."

"So you think it'll be ready for Westinghouse?" Jason was working on an electronic device of some sort that could draw energy from the sun to power space vehicles. He planned to enter it in the Westinghouse Science Talent Search when it was ready. Jason's passion for science was one of the things she loved best about him.

He nodded, then began talking about a problem he'd run into with the experiment. Jenna settled back in her seat and relaxed. She knew he'd be going on about the project for the rest of the bus ride.

When they reached the theater, Jenna was relieved to see that the coming attractions had already begun, which meant she wouldn't have to talk. Not until the movie was over, anyway.

Jason offered her some popcorn, then wedged the container between his knees. If he sensed anything was wrong between them, he didn't let on.

He had asked her to choose the movie, and she had tried to pick something they would both enjoy, finally deciding on a comedy that a lot of their friends had been talking about. But Jenna found it difficult to concentrate. She couldn't stop thinking about the investigation. What was even worse, the film was one of those buddy-cop movies.

Her attention began to wander, coming to rest on a girl who sat in the section across the aisle. She had taken the last seat in her row. Something about the way the girl's body was turned, her back partially pressed against the wall, made her seem on guard. Most of the seats on that side of the room were empty, including all the seats in the row where the girl sat. The majority of people, like Jason and Jenna, had chosen to sit in the middle section.

Jenna wondered if the girl was alone. She couldn't imagine coming to a movie without a friend or a date. It struck her as an incredibly brave thing to do. That was when she suddenly realized that the person she had been staring at all this time was Amy Ruggerio. Jenna's shoulders twitched involuntarily. Amy Ruggerio was two years ahead of her in school. Jenna didn't know her personally but, like everyone else, knew her reputation.

So she wasn't at all surprised to see some guy casually slip in next to her, put his arm around her as if she were his exclusive property, and let his hand slide along her thigh. She wondered if this was Amy's date. Did boys actually *date* Amy Ruggerio? But then she saw Amy stiffen, jerk her leg away from the boy's grasp, and press herself even closer to the wall.

She would have kept watching them, Amy and this boy, who were far more interesting than the movie, if Jason hadn't set the empty popcorn container on the sticky floor and slipped his arm around her shoulders. Loud music blasted out at them from the speakers, followed by an onslaught of gunshots. The screen was ablaze with action. Jenna felt Jason's grip on her shoulder tighten. And that was when her heart began to race all over again.

She would have expected her heart to pound wildly when he touched her, just as it always did. But not like this. This was . . . She stumbled around for the word she wanted. *Fear.* Yes, that was it: fear. Was it possible that her feelings for Jason, a major part of her life for so long, had changed? And changed drastically? She was so stunned by this betrayal, she did not know what to think.

This was a horrible feeling, a feeling so suffocating that she thought she might pass out. Slowly she rose to her feet, mumbled something about the rest room, and stumbled up the aisle, terrified that she might faint in front of all these people.

Once in the rest room, she grabbed hold of the countertop that surrounded the row of sinks and tried to focus on her breathing. Deep breath in. Deep breath out. But it wasn't working. She couldn't seem to get control of her body. She felt dizzy. The room was too bright. She glanced up at the fluorescent light overhead. It hurt her eyes.

Then the light seemed to be moving, swirling, in a kind of black-and-white whirlpool. Her knees could no longer hold her. She was going down, sinking. And there wasn't anything she could do about it.

The hands on her shoulders were strong and competent but somehow gentle, too. They guided her body into a seat, rolling her shoulders forward so that her head was between her knees.

A voice floated above her. "Keep your head down, okay? Try to take a deep breath."

The hands were still on her shoulders, gently working the tight muscles. "Try to relax."

When she dared to open her eyes, Jenna realized she was staring upside down at the porcelain base of a toilet. Stunned, she bolted upright, coming face-to-face with Amy Ruggerio.

"There aren't any paper bags in here. This'll have to do." She handed Jenna a paper towel bunched up with a small opening at one end. "Breathe into this. You need to inhale and exhale in deep breaths."

Jenna did as Amy had instructed, and gradually she began to feel less light-headed.

"You were hyperventilating," Amy told her. "You almost fainted."

Jenna blinked, trying to get her bearings.

Amy stared down at the toilet and shrugged. "Sorry. It's the only place in here where you can sit."

Jenna nodded. "It's okay." Then, as an afterthought, she added, "Thanks."

Amy smiled. She soaked a paper towel with cold water and put it on the back of Jenna's neck. "See if this helps."

The cool water felt good on her skin, which only minutes earlier had prickled with sweat.

"I'll be okay," Jenna told her. "You should get back to your date."

Amy frowned, as if she wasn't at all sure what Jenna was talking about. "I came to the movie alone."

"But that guy . . ." Jenna squeezed her eyes closed. How could she be so stupid? Now Amy would know she'd been watching them.

But Amy didn't seem to notice. She rummaged through her enormous shoulder bag and pulled out a compact. "That *guy*," she informed Jenna, turning to face the mirror, "is not my date. He's a creep." She began to smooth powder over her shiny forehead. "They get these ideas, you know? They hear things and then they think . . ." Amy tossed her free hand in the air, shrugged, and shook her head, as if that said it all.

Jenna watched her pull a lip liner from her bag and go to work on her lips. She wanted to ask Amy if this sort of thing happened to her a lot. But she didn't dare. She had no business prying into Amy's personal life. "I guess I'd better get back."

"Are you sure you feel all right?" Amy turned to look at her; her dark eyes were full of concern.

Jenna noticed how deep those eyes were, so deep you could fall right into them. "I'm fine."

Jason was there waiting for her when she stepped out of the rest room. Amy slipped out behind her. Jenna saw her heading across the lobby and out to the mall. Apparently she was not planning to see the rest of the movie.

Suddenly remembering Jason, Jenna said, "You're missing the movie."

"I was worried about you. What happened?"

Jenna tried to shrug it off. She didn't want him worrying. And she definitely didn't want to tell him what had happened—that for reasons she couldn't explain, even to herself, she sometimes grew panicky when she was near him.

"Maybe I should go home," she said.

He stared at her intently. Suddenly his eyes widened and his mouth fell open. He shook his head. "Jeez, I'm such a moron. I can't believe I took you to that movie, all those people shooting at each other . . . I . . . ."

Jenna gently put her hand over his mouth. "It's okay. It wasn't the movie. Really. Besides, I'm the one who suggested it."

Jason's bony shoulders slumped forward. "We could go to another show," he suggested hopefully.

"Some other time, okay?"

Reluctantly he agreed to take her home, and they headed back to the bus stop. Jenna was grateful that he didn't ask any more questions.

On the bus going home, she began to wonder if her panic around Jason was somehow connected to her father's death.

Maybe she shouldn't be dating anyone right now. She was supposed to be mourning, right? Only so far that hadn't happened. It had been three weeks, and she hadn't once cried. She didn't count the sneaky little tears that sometimes came while she slept.

It was almost dark outside, and the lights in the bus caught her image in the window. She stared back at her reflection and wondered if her father's death was always going to be there, sitting between her and Jason like some massive, unmovable rock.

michael

ichael lay awake almost half the night, as he often did now. When he finally fell asleep, he dreamt he was flying. At first, as he leaned into the wind, arms extended like wings, the sensation of the air lifting him was exhilarating. He imagined this was how a bird felt, as light as feathery seeds released from their pods, floating gently on a breeze. He soared upward into the sky, never once fearing he would fall. He flew over treetops and rooftops, over fields and gardens, until his body suddenly curved in an arc and headed toward the earth. Then he saw the man below on the roof. And that was when Michael knew he was not a bird at all. He was, in fact, a bullet.

Frantically he twisted his body to the right, then to the left, but it stayed on course no matter how hard he tried to steer it away. His body began to pick up speed as it headed downward. Faster and faster, it streaked toward the unsuspecting man on the roof.

Michael tried to scream a warning. He tried to get the man to move, to get out of the way. But no sound came from his burning throat. It was going to happen, and he could do nothing to stop it.

Michael managed to wake himself just as the top of his

head was about to strike the man's skull. He lay in a damp pool of sweat, barely able to breathe. His heart was pounding so loudly the sound of it filled his ears, blocking out the soft chirping of the crickets. He gripped the edges of his bed and held on until his heart began to quiet and he was able to take a deep breath.

He knew this was happening because he had seen Jenna Ward at the pool earlier that day. He had stared across the pool into her face and suddenly realized there would never be anyplace on earth where he could hide.

At first he had wanted to believe that the person dangling her feet in the water merely resembled Jenna Ward. So while he automatically moved his head from side to side, pretending to keep a sharp eye on the swimmers, he studied her from behind the metallic shield of his sunglasses. There could be no doubt. It was Jenna Ward. No one else had eyes like hers. Those eyes had haunted him from the moment he first saw her picture in the newspaper.

Until that morning he had been secure in his belief that the Wards were not members of the community pool. It had never occurred to him that Jenna or her mother might come as someone's guest. But when Jenna had shown up, all he had been able to think about for the rest of the day was how he was going to make it through the summer if she continued to come to the pool.

Now, as the cicadas buzzed loudly beneath his window, his mind once again searched in vain for a way out of all this. He thought of quitting his job. But he needed the money. He could look for other work. But it was late in the summer and all the seasonal jobs were already taken. And deep down, he knew working someplace else wouldn't protect him from running into Jenna Ward. She could show up anywhere. Anytime.

The glare from the streetlight outside spilled across the lower part of his bed. It was still dark. The air in his room was stifling. Michael glanced over at the digital clock. It was only a little after three. He knew it was pointless to lie there. He wouldn't be able to sleep. So he kicked aside the damp sheet. And because he usually slept naked on hot, humid nights, he slipped on a pair of boxer shorts.

When he reached the bottom of the stairs, he was startled by muffled sounds coming from the TV. Someone was up, although the house was completely dark except for the muted light coming from the television screen. He hesitated, worried that it might be his father or mother. They would question him, wonder what he was doing up so late.

Finally he crept into the kitchen. If he was quiet enough, they might not discover he was up. But as he stood in the middle of the dark room, he couldn't think of why he had come there. He wasn't hungry. He didn't want anything to drink. What had he planned to do? Watch television, maybe. But now he couldn't. He thought about going out on the patio. At least it would be cooler outside. But just as he reached for the doorknob the overhead fluorescent light blinked on.

Josh stood in the doorway, wearing only his baggy pajama bottoms, his arms folded. "Are you sleepwalking?"

Michael was so stunned by the sudden appearance of the light and then Josh that he merely shook his head and let his hand fall away from the knob.

"Because if you are, I'm not supposed to wake you." Josh moved cautiously toward his brother. "I'm supposed to take your hand and lead you back to bed."

"I'm awake," Michael told him.

"You don't act like you're awake." Josh took a step back

and studied his brother's face. "Where do you think you're going?"

"Outside."

"In your underwear?" Josh rolled his eyes toward the ceiling and made clicking noises with his tongue. "The neighbors'll think you're a pervert."

"It's three o'clock in the morning, you little dork. Who's going to see me?" This whole conversation was ridiculous. Why was he even arguing with Josh? He didn't owe him any explanations. Michael stared down at him. "What are you doing up so late, anyway?"

"It's summer." Josh was obviously annoyed that the pressure was now on him. "I can stay up as late as I want."

Michael noticed his brother was still carrying the remote control. "And that's when all the best R-rated movies are on cable, right?"

In the fluorescent light it was difficult to tell whether Josh had turned a shade paler, but Michael was sure he had. He nodded at his brother. "Right. I figured as much."

Josh sat down at the kitchen table and laid the remote in front of him. "So what? I like to see naked girls. So what?"

Michael opened the refrigerator and pulled out a carton of milk. What could he say? He liked to look at naked women, too. He wasn't going to be a hypocrite about it. He took a swallow of milk right from the carton.

Josh kept watching him, but he didn't say anything. Michael handed him the carton. Josh took a swallow. It was as if they had made a silent pact and were now sealing it.

Michael pulled a package of Oreos from the cupboard and tossed it on the table, then brought out two glasses and filled them with milk. For a while the two of them just sat there dunking cookies silently until Josh, his teeth speckled with dark crumbs, said suddenly, "Hey, did you hear the cops are about to nail Charlie Ward's killer?"

The lump of white icing Michael had licked off his cookie suddenly stuck in his throat. "How do you know that?"

"I heard Dad talking about it with Mr. Epel next door." Josh looked pleased that he could tell his brother something he didn't know. "Mr. Epel said the cops showed up at the Finleys' house two blocks over. They were going door-to-door asking people questions."

Michael fought to keep the panic out of his voice. "Why this neighborhood?"

Josh tilted his head to the side and stared up at the ceiling, trying to recall more of the conversation between Mr. Epel and his father. "Well, Mr. Epel said he heard that the ballistics team had narrowed down the area where the bullet came from to four blocks."

It was all true, then. The nightmare was real. Michael could no longer pretend, as he sometimes did, that there was a chance he hadn't fired that fatal shot. The bullet had come from somewhere in his neighborhood. The chances of someone else in such a small area shooting off a gun around noon on that same day were probably one in a million. He had spent weeks trying to get used to the idea that he had committed this hideous act. But always, somewhere, there had been hope. A bullet traveling a mile or more through the air could have come from as far away as the next town over. There had always been the outside chance that someone else had fired a gun into the air that Fourth of July afternoon. Now that chance no longer existed.

"Are you saying our block is one of the four?" Michael's

words felt slow and labored. Part of him didn't want the answer to that question.

Josh shrugged and reached for another cookie. "The cops aren't saying which blocks." He popped the whole cookie into his mouth. "Why would they?" he said, spraying crumbs as he talked. "I mean, jeez, nothing like alerting the murderer in case he wants to beat feet or anything. They're just gonna show up at your front door and . . . *surprise!*" he shouted, leaning his body across the table and spitting chocolate crumbs in Michael's face.

Michael wanted to punch him right in the mouth, but he had both hands clamped tightly around the sides of his chair, trying to ground himself.

Josh narrowed his eyes at his brother. "So, been doing any target practice lately? You know, with that rifle Grandpa gave you on your birthday?" A snide grin spread across his face.

Michael stared him down. "Are you trying to say I shot Charlie Ward?" Michael was gripping the edge of his chair for dear life. But he managed to keep his voice calm. Each word came out carefully weighted.

Josh backed off, aware that he'd gone too far. "Hey, I was just kidding."

"You don't kid about something like that."

Not wanting to get himself in any deeper, Josh picked up the remote and headed for the door. "Want to come watch TV?" Michael knew this was his brother's way of trying to get back on his good side.

So after a few minutes had passed—and because he had nowhere else to go—Michael followed Josh into the living room, and for the next three hours he stared at the flashing images on the television screen without seeing one single thing.

In spite of his best efforts, his pledge not to impose on her, Michael found himself gravitating back to Amy's house on lonely, hot nights. Nights when even the bats flew too slowly to catch their quota of mosquitoes. On those nights he cocooned himself in Amy's overstuffed living room and played Monopoly or Scrabble. Sometimes they watched rented videos or made Rice Krispies squares. But they never went out anywhere.

Michael had learned a lot about Amy and her family during those weeks. He learned that her mother and father had died in a car accident when Amy was only seven, that Amy had been in the car but had survived, although she had a broken leg and fractured ribs. He also found out that her father's parents had taken Amy in and raised her, and that Pappy was her only living relative.

On some nights her grandfather watched a movie with them or joined them in a game of Scrabble. Michael liked Pappy. He was a short, wiry man with milky blue eyes, thick white hair, and a goatee that looked like a soft wad of cotton. And he invented such ridiculous words when they played Scrabble that it was easy for them to challenge him, which didn't bother Pappy in the least. He thought the only real fun in playing the game was making up crazy words.

But on other nights, when Pappy went next door to Tony Rico's house to play a few hands of poker with his friends or took a stack of back issues of *Popular Mechanics* upstairs to read in bed, Michael and Amy would sit in the dark with only the flickering light from the TV splashing colors on Amy's face. And Michael would move a little farther away from her on the couch. Because if he didn't, he would have reached for her. He would have circled his arms around her waist and slid her down on the cushions. But he wouldn't allow himself to do that. If he did, he would have to admit he was using Amy. Admit that she was allowing herself to be used. Then he would have to stop coming to her house. He had already taken enough.

But on this particular night in late July, Michael found that even sitting on the floor across from Amy, drinking root beer and playing Scrabble, was not enough to quiet his mind. No one had shown up at his front door yet, but he knew it could happen any day if what Josh said was true.

"I don't think *quitch* is a word," Amy told him.

Michael stared down at the board. The Scrabble piece he was holding felt sticky. "Are you going to challenge it?" he asked.

Amy watched him closely, as if she was trying to gauge his mood. "Well, it *is* a triple word score. That's a lot of points."

"So challenge it." He was hardly able to keep the irritation out of his voice, although he knew it wasn't Amy he was upset with.

Amy stared down at her lap. She was sitting cross-legged on one of the couch cushions they had put on the floor. "I guess it could be a real word. I mean, I'm not doubting you or anything."

"Jeez, Amy. This is a game. People make up words if they think they can get away with it." Michael swung his hands out, palms up. "They want to win!" He reached over and snapped up the dictionary from the coffee table. "Doubt me," he said, handing it to her.

Amy took the dictionary without looking at him. She seemed to take a long time fumbling through the pages. Then Michael noticed the surprised flutter of her dark lashes, and when she looked up, her delight was so open and childlike that he wanted to grab her by the shoulders and shake her until she understood. He was not to be trusted.

"It's a real word," she said softly. "I should have believed you."

Michael's jaw tightened. He had had no idea that *quitch* was a real word. He thought he had made it up. He took the dictionary from her. Sure enough, there it was. Quitch was a kind of grasslike weed. He closed the book and let it rest heavily in his lap. Finally he said, "I thought I made it up."

"But it's okay, because you didn't."

"No, it's not okay. I was trying to cheat." Michael was growing agitated. He needed to get away from Amy. "Look," he said, getting to his feet, "I'm pretty tired tonight. We'll finish this some other time, all right?"

Amy didn't say anything. She lifted the Scrabble board from the floor, careful not to jar any of the letters, and gently set it on the coffee table.

Michael was already walking toward the door. Amy crossed the room and stood in front of him. She rested the palm of her hand against his chest, as if she were trying to feel his heartbeat. "You never try to kiss me," she whispered, keeping her eyes on her hand.

Michael's body tensed, filling with desire. He told himself that he did not want this to happen. He told himself that Amy was just a good friend.

"That time in your garage," Amy said. "At your birthday party . . ." She sucked in her breath, as if that might give her the extra courage to somehow get through this. "Didn't you like kissing me?"

"Sure." Michael covered her hand, the one still touching his chest, with his own. He could feel the chemistry between them. His heart was racing.

"Then why?"

He thought of Darcy suddenly. She had been in Ocean City with her parents for two weeks. But she was supposed to have gotten home that day. Michael wasn't at all sure what Darcy would do if she found out he'd been spending so much time with Amy. Probably break up with him. And really, wasn't that what he wanted? Wouldn't it be easier for her if she was the one to break it off? Still . . .

"Amy . . . ," he began, about to remind her of Darcy. But she was looking up at him now. Waiting. Suddenly there didn't seem to be anything he could say. He leaned forward, pulling her body as close to his as he could, breathing in the scent of her hair, brushing his lips against her ear, her eyelid, her cheek, as if he could never get enough of her. And as his lips came to rest on hers he realized he'd been fooling himself all along. Now, for the first time, he admitted to himself how much he really wanted her.

"Amy," he whispered, "I have to go now." If he stayed another minute, it would be too late. He reached behind her and fumbled with the doorknob.

Amy had her head tilted to one side, watching him, as if she was trying to understand something. "Then go," she said simply, stepping aside and helping him to push the door open wider.

Each casual step down the front walk cost him; the strain of keeping his body loose and unhurried was unbearable. He would have run if Amy hadn't still been standing at the door.

How had he let this happen? Darcy was probably back and waiting for his call. He had enough problems to deal with. The last thing he needed was to get tangled up with another girl. And not just any girl, Amy Ruggerio. Yet even as her name entered his thoughts the intense feeling he had experienced at her front door only moments earlier spread through his body like wildfire.

He took a deep breath. Whatever was going to happen would happen. There was no point in fighting it. He understood that now. Because this was a world where things you never thought could happen to you did. And where you didn't always get to choose your fate, or the people you loved. Sometimes it just happened.

a few days later Michael took another driver's test. This time he passed. At least he could put an end to that small web of deceit, although it brought him little relief. Other webs had already sprung up in its place.

Since Darcy had returned from Ocean City, Michael had somehow managed to put their relationship on hold, talking with her only at the pool or on the phone. But it had been more than a week and she was growing impatient.

When Darcy finally did confront him, it was just as he was leaving work. She was sitting on the hood of her father's Taurus, sipping slowly from a bottle of natural spring water. Michael's first thought was that the hood of the car had to be about five hundred degrees. He wondered how she could sit there so patiently, looking so deliciously cool in her red shorts and flowered top. Her sandaled feet hung over the side, exposing her bare thighs to the scorching metal. And she never even flinched, just lifted her hand and waved him over.

Michael came to stand in front of her. Waiting. He knew what was coming. It had been coming for weeks.

"You haven't said anything about Kim Cohen's party,"

Darcy said, taking another swallow of water. "I just wondered if we were still going." Her lips were stretched in a tight smile.

When Michael didn't say anything, she added, "It's tonight, remember?"

He felt the familiar thickness in his throat when he looked into her soft hazel eyes. "Darcy," he began, his voice husky. But she held up her hand to stop him.

"Wait, let me guess," she said. "You've had a tough day at the pool and you're too tired to party, right?" She slid off the hood of the car. The soles of her sandals smacked against the blacktop. "You're starting to sound just like my dad."

"It's not like that."

"Fine. Tell me what it is, then." She emptied the bottle and tossed it into the backseat of the car.

Michael took her hand and held it for a minute, rubbing his thumb back and forth across her smooth skin. How could he tell her that he couldn't be around her right now? He didn't want to be around anyone. It was too difficult. Even being around Amy was hard.

"It's not you," he said softly, staring down at the light freckles that covered the back of her hand. "It's me. My life is really screwed up right now."

"It's true, then," Darcy said, snatching her hand away from him.

Michael thought his heart had stopped. He wondered if she could have possibly found out he had killed a man. He shook his head, fighting to keep his face expressionless. "What's true?"

"That you've been getting it on with the slut."

It took him a few seconds to realize Darcy was talking about Amy. "I'm not 'getting it on' with anyone," he said, trying to keep the mounting anger out of his voice.

Darcy yanked open the door of her father's car and climbed behind the wheel. "We saw you."

"Who saw me? What are you talking about?" Michael's fingers gripped the top of the car door, keeping her from closing it. He knew he and Amy had never gone anywhere together. No one could have seen them.

Darcy gave the car door a futile tug, but Michael held on. With an angry snort, she shoved the key in the ignition and started the engine. "Allison, Kim, and I were out driving around the night I got back. We saw you."

"Saw me what?"

"Saw you turn down Amy's street."

"So?" He wondered how Darcy or the others had known it was Amy's street. "I was out walking. Big deal."

Darcy stared down at the steering wheel. Her long red hair fell forward, hiding her profile. "Do you think I don't know something's wrong, Mike? I mean, we hardly ever see each other anymore."

Then it came to him, like a rush of hot air from an open oven door. It all but slapped him in the face. "You were spying on me," he said, his voice barely audible because the full weight of this fact hadn't quite sunk in yet.

"I had to know if you were seeing someone else." Darcy lifted her chin defensively. "*You* sure as hell weren't going to tell me."

"You and your friends were tailing me." He shook his head in disbelief.

Darcy had begun to cry. Tiny ribbons of mascara snaked down her cheeks.

Michael reached down and turned off the ignition, then came around to the other side of the car and climbed into the passenger seat. Darcy's hands were clamped around the steering wheel as if she were holding on for dear life, and all the while she kept up her steady hiccuplike sobbing.

"It's not what you think," he told her. "Amy and I are just friends."

Darcy hiccupped another sob. "Oh, right." She swatted at the brown streaks on her cheeks. "What kind of an idiot do you think I am?"

"You don't have to believe me," he said. "I just wanted you to know. It has nothing to do with you. With us."

Darcy slit her eyes at him. "Get out of my car."

This was not how he wanted to leave her. In fact, he really wasn't sure if he even wanted to leave her. Everything was so screwed up. Still, it had finally come to this. There was no way around it without confessing everything.

For one brief moment he thought of telling her the truth. He tried to imagine how Darcy would react. Would she try to comfort him? Tell him Charlie Ward's death was an accident? Would she tell the police?

Would he be telling her the truth just to save her pride? And what would that buy him? He knew he couldn't go on seeing her, anyway. Because this breakup wasn't about Amy or Darcy; it was about carrying a secret so terrible that it shut him off from the rest of the world.

Michael unfolded himself from the passenger seat and came to stand by her window as Darcy started up the engine again. "Why her?" she said as she began to back up. "That's what I'd like to know. Is it because I said I wasn't ready yet? You couldn't wait?"

"Darcy." He almost moaned her name.

"She's such a pig."

Michael surprised himself by reaching into the slowly moving car and grabbing Darcy by the shoulder. Her foot hit the brake instinctively, and the car rocked back and forth. "Amy Ruggerio is one of the most decent human beings I know," he said, clenching his teeth. "She's been a good friend to me. A friend, period. You can believe whatever the hell you want. But nobody calls a friend of mine—any friend of mine—a pig."

Darcy gave him a look of pure hatred. Then she lowered her jaw to his hand and, before he had time to react, bit him as hard as she could. When Michael yanked his hand back, startled, Darcy stepped on the gas and peeled out of the parking lot, spitting tiny stones from beneath the tires of the Taurus.

He stared down at his throbbing hand. She hadn't broken the skin, but he had no doubt that she would have if he hadn't pulled away when he did. He didn't blame Darcy, although he was badly shaken by her behavior. After all, he had made a complete mess of things. He hadn't been honest with her. What was she supposed to think?

Still rubbing his sore hand, he watched her tear down the road. Then, because there was nothing else he could do about Darcy, he headed for the library. He still went almost every night to see if there were any new developments in the Ward case, especially now. He knew the police had continued going door-to-door the past week. So far they had not been on his street.

It occurred to him, as he climbed the stone steps to the building, that he had *wanted* Darcy to be the one to end their relationship. He had let it come to that. As he reached for the doorknob he saw the deep tooth marks in his hand and the swollen, red skin. If he had stayed with her, he would have only hurt her even more in the end, when the truth finally came out.

The end, he knew, would come when the authorities discovered that all their evidence pointed to one killer: Michael MacKenzie. And even though Joe was still convinced they were both practically in the clear, Michael knew better. He knew it was only a matter of time.

The night the police came to the MacKenzies' front door was the same night a renegade tornado tore the rooftops off fourteen units in the apartment complex behind the A&P. It peeled them right off like an old brown banana skin, and no one saw it coming.

On that particular night in early August, the sky was the color of an oxidized penny and the air was deathly still. Michael answered the door because his mother was at the mall and his father and Josh were right in the middle of *Jeopardy!* Even a tornado advisory, had it been bleeped in bold white letters across the bottom of the screen, would not have interrupted their game.

Michael knew the two men who stared back at him through the screen door. The younger, dressed in jeans and a T-shirt, was Doug Boyle. He had been with the police force for only a year. Michael and his friends had nicknamed him the Hangman because he made his reputation catching kids who were drinking in the park, then booking them. Sometimes he waited, patient as a cat, in alleyways between the shops in town so that he could nail kids for speeding down Main Street.

The older man, a man about Michael's father's age, wearing khaki slacks and a madras shirt, was Ralph Healey. He'd
been a sergeant on the police force as long as Michael could
remember.

At the sight of them, Michael's body grew rigid. He stared
at the two men as if they had just announced their plans to
torch the MacKenzie house and everyone in it.

"We need to ask you and your family a few questions,
Mike," Sergeant Healey said. He had his head tipped slightly to
the side, eyes narrowed. Michael knew he was being sized up.

"They're watching *Jeopardy!*" Michael said, acutely aware
of how stupid he must sound.

"It'll take only a couple of minutes," Healey assured him.
"Strictly routine."

And because there didn't seem to be any other course of
action, Michael stepped back and let them in.

Josh was so engrossed in his program that he didn't even
look up when they entered the living room. "Just talk loud," he
told everyone, not bothering to turn the sound down on the TV.
But as soon as the men announced they were there about the
Ward case, he grabbed the remote and the TV screen went
blank.

Michael thought about going up to his room and letting
his father handle the police, but he was afraid it might look
suspicious. Besides, Ralph Healey had said he wanted to talk to
all of them. So Michael took an inconspicuous seat in the corner of the room. Josh merely stayed in the same place on the
floor, except that he now faced the other direction.

Doug Boyle made himself at home on the couch without
being asked, but Sergeant Healey extended his hand, squeezing
Tom MacKenzie's in a hearty shake. "Sorry about the intrusion."

"Forget it. Have a seat." Michael's father pointed to the empty space next to Doug Boyle. "I heard you guys have been asking questions around the neighborhood."

Ralph Healey leaned forward, hands folded, elbows balanced on his thick knees, and nodded. "The guys from Picatinny finally zeroed in on the area where the bullet was fired from. They narrowed it down to four blocks."

"So you think somebody from this neighborhood shot that gun?" Tom MacKenzie rubbed the palms of his hands along his thighs.

Healey looked grim. "Well, it sure looks that way," he said. "That's why we're here. We've been doing the rest of the investigation on foot. Asking the folks around here a few questions."

Michael's father stared down at the carpet but didn't say anything.

Michael was suddenly aware of every muscle in his body, as if he were readying himself for an explosive takeoff from the starting block at a track meet. All his senses were attuned to Healey's every word, his every move. Waiting.

Ralph Healey had rough red hands. He kept them folded, fingers locked, as if he were about to pray. Michael found the image disturbing. "I guess you've been following the case in the papers," Healey said to Michael's father.

"Everyone in town has," Josh volunteered. "I mean, man, this is *so* cool. A murder right here in Briarwood." Then he looked over his shoulder at Michael and gave him a sly grin, hinting that he knew something. Michael wanted to punch his lights out. Meanwhile the three men were staring down at Josh as if he had just surfaced from somewhere beneath the carpet.

Tom MacKenzie glared at Josh. "I hardly think someone dying, especially the way Charlie Ward did, could be described as cool."

Watching his father and brother, Michael was suddenly aware that his father had not looked his way even once since the police had entered the room. It was as if he weren't even there. Such behavior was so out of character for his father that Michael began to wonder if he suspected something.

"You guys have any ideas about what kind of gun it was?" Tom MacKenzie asked, turning his attention back to the two men.

When Healey didn't say anything, Doug Boyle slid his wide backside forward on the couch, as if he'd just decided to be part of the investigation. "We can't give out that information," he said.

"We're just asking people if they have any handguns or rifles in their houses or if they know of anybody in the neighborhood who does." Ralph Healey parted his hands apologetically. "It's nasty business, asking people to point fingers. But if you know of anybody . . ."

"A lot of people around here have rifles," Tom MacKenzie said. "I don't know about handguns." He frowned, looking skeptical. "I've got two rifles of my own." Then he cocked his head toward Michael. "And Mike's got an old .45-70 Winchester his grandfather gave him."

Michael's heart raced uncontrollably. A light sheen of sweat appeared on his upper lip and forehead. He was sure someone would notice.

Ralph Healey eased his body back into the couch, as if he could relax now that he'd gotten what he'd come for. He sighed and looked toward the picture window. "I'll need to see those rifles," he said. Then added, "Nothing personal. We have to inspect everyone's guns."

Michael watched as his father stood up, hands in pockets. He could tell his father had been caught off guard by the sergeant's request. Then he turned to Michael for the first time since the police had shown up. "Better go get the Winchester," he said.

Maybe it was something about the way his father said this, but in that single moment Michael realized with horror that his father had at least considered the possibility that the shot had come from his own house.

Michael licked his lips. "It's not here," he said, surprised by the evenness of his own voice.

His father stared back at him, hands still in his pockets. He shook his head as if he hadn't heard right. "Where is it?"

Without a moment's hesitation, Michael said, "At Joe's."

His father continued shaking his head. He seemed bewildered. "What's it doing at Joe's?"

Michael kept his eyes on his father's face. He was afraid that if he looked away, the gesture would scream his guilt. He shrugged as casually as he could, although the muscles in his shoulders and neck ached with tension. "I loaned it to him."

Tom MacKenzie yanked a hand from his pocket and jerked his thumb in the direction of the cordless phone. "Well, call him and tell him to get it over here."

Michael could see that his father was upset. He couldn't be sure if it was only because his son had loaned out the rifle or because he sensed something else. Michael picked up the phone and dialed Joe Sadowski's number. He wasn't worried. He knew Joe was at work. All he'd have to do was leave a message. But to his horror, Joe answered.

"I thought you'd be at work," Michael said, forgetting the others who stood only a few feet away.

"I got fired."

Michael knew he should ask him what happened, but this was not the time. Somehow he had to pull this thing off. And he had to make Joe play along. "Listen, I need my rifle back."

The silence lasted so long he was afraid Joe had hung up. "What in—? Man, I don't have your rifle."

"Oh, man, you're kidding, right? Why didn't you tell me before?" Michael said. "My dad's gonna be pissed."

"About what? I don't have your goddamn rifle." Joe drew a deep breath. "Man, you're losing it. You're really losing it."

"Jesus, they stole it right out of the car?" The desperation in Michael's voice was convincing. He *was* desperate. But not for the reasons the men standing behind him in the living room believed.

"Tell him to find the damn gun and get over here," Tom MacKenzie said loudly. "Now!"

"Was that your old man?" Joe asked. "He's standing right there? What the—?"

Michael looked over at his father. "He can't, Dad. It was stolen."

Tom MacKenzie raked his fingers through his hair. "Stolen? Who the hell stole it?"

"He doesn't know. It was in the backseat of his car. Somebody broke in, took his CD player and the rifle."

Ralph Healey took a step forward, coming within a foot of Michael. "Did he file a report?"

"Who was that?" Joe said from the other end of the phone. "That wasn't your dad."

"I don't know, Mr. Healey," Michael said. Then to Joe, "Did you notify the police?"

"The *cops* are there? Oh, man. Oh, man, we're screwed."

Michael kept his gaze steady as he looked at Healey. "He says it just happened last night. He hasn't had a chance to file a report yet."

"Mike?" Joe's voice was barely audible.

"Yeah?"

"Meet me at the park in an hour." Then he hung up.

Michael pushed the Off button on the phone and laid it carefully on the table. "I can't believe he didn't tell me before now," he said.

"That Winchester belonged to your grandfather when he was a boy," his father said. Michael could see he was angry.

"Dad, I'm sorry."

"What in hell were you thinking? Loaning that gun to an idiot like Sadowski."

Ralph Healey interjected a light cough. "Well, maybe you could just show us those other two rifles for now," he said to Tom MacKenzie. Then he turned to Michael. "Don't worry about your Winchester. We'll track it down."

by the time Michael left for the park, the tornado had already struck and moved on. The rain that followed lasted for only fifteen minutes. And then it was all over.

The public park next to the library was where most of the kids from Briarwood Regional hung out during the summer months. Joe was already there when Michael arrived. He found him sitting on an empty pizza box beneath a gnarled old sycamore several yards from where most of the other kids were gathered. Joe held out a half-empty can of beer in greeting. Michael shook his head and stared down at the wet grass in front of him. Joe pulled the box from beneath him, tore off the top, and handed it to his friend. "Found this over there," he said, pointing to a nearby trash can. Then he sat back on the half of the box that remained.

Michael lowered himself onto the cardboard. He had

spent the past few weeks avoiding Joe. And yet, when he'd had nowhere else to turn, this was the person he had called. He realized now that by making up the theft story, he had dragged Joe even further into the dark mire that threatened to swallow them both up.

"What did you do with it?" Joe asked. The red bandanna he had rolled up and tied around his head was dark with sweat.

Michael didn't have to ask what he meant. "Hid it where nobody's ever going to find it."

"Where?"

The mosquitoes were biting furiously. Michael wished he had sprayed himself with insect repellent before he'd left the house. He shook his head. "It's better if you don't know."

"How come the cops showed up at your house?"

"They're checking out everyone within a four-block radius." He slapped hard at a mosquito. The smack left a red imprint of his fingers on his arm. "The ballistics experts narrowed it down to our neighborhood."

Joe took a swallow of beer and stared down at the can thoughtfully. "They'll be coming to my house, too, then." When Michael didn't answer, he added, "We got to get this stolen gun story straight."

Michael tugged at the wet grass with his hand, pulling thin blades loose from the soil. "You don't have to do this, you know."

Joe put his hand on Michael's shoulder and leaned into his face. "So what you're saying is, when the cops come to my house it's okay to tell them you made up that whole stolen gun thing so they wouldn't find out you're the one who fired the shot?"

Michael stared down at Joe's hand. He felt the weight of it. "Yeah," he said, "go ahead. Tell them that." And he meant it.

Joe smacked him lightly on the side of the head. "I was yanking your chain, you moron. Lighten up."

Michael felt the full impact of that playful slap. Not the physical pain of it; there was none. What he felt was the desperation behind it. The desperation to keep things the way they had always been between them. And to that end, he was sure, Joe would stand by him, tell the lies Michael asked him to tell, risk whatever lay ahead for both of them. A risk, Michael knew, his friend did not have to take. And he could not help wondering, in that moment, if he would have been willing to do the same for Joe.

"Hey, man. No matter what, you're pretty much home free," Joe said. "They can't prove anything without the weapon. If they got any evidence at all, it's circumstantial."

Michael stared up at the old sycamore behind Joe. The base was almost four feet in diameter and had three trunks growing from it. It reminded him of the Ghost Tree, but it wasn't as big. He hadn't thought about that place in years, although he and Joe used to hang out there as kids and tell each other horror stories about the Great Swamp Devil. He thought of that now, sitting across from Joe. The difference was that the horror story they shared this time was real.

"Well?" Joe was studying him closely.

"Well what?"

"So what do you want me to tell the cops?" He took another long gulp of beer.

Michael shrugged. "Same thing I did. That you borrowed the gun a few days ago, and last night somebody broke into your car and stole it."

"Along with my CD player," Joe added. "No problem."

Joe's eyes were unusually bright, his face flushed. Michael

had the sudden disconcerting thought that his friend was actually enjoying all this.

The dampness was seeping through the cardboard. Michael stood up, remembering suddenly that Joe had lost his job. "How'd you manage to get fired?" he asked.

Joe chugged the rest of his beer and held up the can. "I was having a little refreshment in the men's room on my break."

"They caught you drinking on the job?" Michael shook his head.

"No, man. They caught me drinking on my break."

Michael picked up the soggy cardboard and glanced over at the trash can. His preoccupation kept him from having to look at the snide grin on Joe's face. "So what are you going to do now?" He began to fold the cardboard into a smaller square.

Joe shrugged. "We still got a few weeks left before school starts," he said. "Might as well enjoy them."

Michael had taken only a few steps toward the trash can when he spotted the police car by the drive-up book drop in front of the library. Doug Boyle, now in his regular uniform, was crossing the park to where a group of kids sat in a tight circle, playing cards by flashlight.

Joe had seen him, too. He crushed the beer can with his foot and kicked it into the bushes. "I'll call you later," he told Michael, heading toward the sidewalk. Then he cocked his head in the direction of Doug Boyle. "Well, move it, man. You just going to stand there?" He shook his head in disbelief. "Haven't you seen enough of the Hangman for one night?"

The next morning Joe went to the police station to file a report. Michael did not go with him because he had to be at work by nine. But Joe told him later that afternoon, as they stood in the parking lot at the community pool, that he'd taken care of everything. He had even removed the CD player from the car the night before and hidden it in an old trunk in the attic in case the police wanted to inspect his Mustang.

"Oh, yeah, and I threw in about how they took all my CDs." Joe leaned back against his car and folded his arms.

Michael stood in the parking lot, still in his bathing trunks, a towel hanging around his neck like a yoke. "So now what?" He had the feeling they had left something undone. Something that would lead the police right to them.

Joe climbed into the front seat of his car and rolled down the window. "Now all I have to do is answer the questions when the cops come to my house."

And the police did come. They showed up that same evening. After they left, Joe drove over to Michael's house. He was so hyper, Michael thought he'd have to tie him down. "I'm revved, man," Joe told him, hopping back and forth like a prizefighter. "Lying to cops has got to be one of the best natural highs in the world."

They were standing on the MacKenzies' front lawn. Michael glanced back at his house. Most of the windows were wide open. "Why don't you just shout it a little louder in case the people over on the next block didn't hear?"

Joe's shoulders fell forward in an awkward slump. He stopped bouncing and stared at Michael. "Is this the face of gratitude?"

Michael headed for the sidewalk, then took off in the direction of the Little League field, which was three blocks away. Joe ran to catch up. "Nobody heard," he said. "And even if they did, they wouldn't know what I was talking about."

Michael stuffed his hands in the pockets of his cutoffs. His body was thrust forward, as if he were about to lunge off a diving board. He kept walking, although he had no idea where he was going.

"Man, you are *really* getting paranoid," Joe said, panting with the effort to keep up.

"What did the cops ask you?" Michael said, changing the subject.

"Probably the same stuff they asked you. They wanted to know if we had any handguns or rifles in the house." Joe laughed. "My old man said nobody in his family had any guns. Said he wouldn't have them in the house. He nearly went ballistic when the Hangman asked about the rifle I'd borrowed from you." Joe held up his index finger. "Wait. Make that 'allegedly' borrowed."

"What'd you tell them?" Michael was walking even faster now.

Joe pressed his palm on Michael's shoulder, trying to

make him slow his pace. "Just like we planned. I told them neither of us ever had a chance to try the rifle out before it got stolen. I told them the last person who fired it was probably your grandfather."

They had come as far as the Little League field. For a few minutes the two of them watched the game in silence. Michael wondered if Joe remembered the year they had played for the Briarwood Bobcats and had an undefeated season. Together, on the same team—as they had constantly reminded each other for years afterward—they were unbeatable.

Michael rested his hands on the metal rail at the top of the chain-link fence and looked on as a boy hit a ground ball to center field, then took off into the wind, spraying dust from the heels of his sneakers. For one anguished moment Michael wanted to be that boy. He would have given anything to trade places with him. That boy had nothing more on his mind than whether or not he would make it to first base.

Joe threw his weight against the fence, rattling the metal links. "I'm telling you, it went fine."

"They got him," Michael said, still staring out at the field.

"What?"

"The kid. They nailed him sliding into first."

ichael had not been to Amy's house since he had broken up with Darcy. So when he did show up, five nights later, he was surprised to find Amy sitting on the front steps, her face blotchy and tearstained. When she saw him coming, she stood up so quickly that she almost lost her balance, then stumbled inside, closing the door behind her. Michael froze at the end of the driveway, unsure what to do next.

He stared up at the sky. Overhead the bats performed their nightly maneuvers, filling their bellies with mosquitoes while negotiating sharp turns and somehow never colliding with each other. Humans, he thought, would probably never learn the art of avoiding collision. Somehow, when people came together, there was always wreckage of some kind left behind. People were messy that way.

It crossed his mind that maybe Amy had found out about his role in the Ward accident, but he knew better. His gut told him her behavior had something to do with Darcy and her friends. He felt this as surely as he had felt Darcy's bite on his hand, although it had been a few days since they had broken up and only the sickly yellow of a faded bruise still tainted his skin.

Michael took a cautious step toward the house. Then another. He couldn't just turn and walk away, leaving more wreckage in his wake. When Amy didn't answer the door, he wedged himself between the junipers in front of the house and called to her through the open window. The sharp needles from the evergreens left tiny red welts on his skin. But he would not leave until he found out what had happened. He shouted that he would sit on her front stairs for the entire night if he had to.

When the door finally opened, it was Pappy who stood in front of him.

"My granddaughter doesn't want to see you." Pappy's voice sounded raspier than usual. His milky blue eyes seemed far away. Having dutifully delivered the message, he started to close the door.

"What did I do?" Michael asked. "Did she tell you?"

Pappy shook his head. "She's not talking." He tipped forward on the balls of his feet, his forehead almost touching the screen, and whispered, "But you hurt her bad, son. Whatever it was you did."

"Tell her I'm not leaving till I see her." Michael knew he sounded desperate, but he didn't care.

Pappy turned around and mumbled something. Then he walked away, leaving the door open. Michael was tempted to step inside, but he knew he wasn't welcome, so he stayed put. He could hear the soft rumblings of their voices coming from the living room. Then Amy was there, standing on the other side of the screen door. Her face was not as splotchy as earlier. She pressed the fingertips of one hand against the screen. She did not invite him in.

Michael was aware that more than a screen door stood between them. He wanted nothing more than to be inside, sitting beside her on the overstuffed couch. Suddenly the thought of losing this tiny sanctuary was just too much to swallow. He had to make at least one thing right in his life. He placed his hand against the screen so that his fingers touched hers. "Tell me what's wrong," he said.

Amy jerked her hand away, the reflex action of someone who has just burned her fingers on a hot stove. "Go home, Michael," she said. Her voice sounded hoarse.

"Amy, whatever it is, let's talk about it."

She had taken a step back, and her hand was on the edge of the door. He could tell she was getting ready to shut him out. "Amy," he said, "does this have anything to do with Darcy?"

The tears that welled up in her eyes told him that it did. "Look," he said, "I can explain."

But Amy only shook her head. "I can't talk about this now. Please go home." And when she shut the door, it was not with a slam but with the heavy clunk of something ending.

A few days later Michael learned from Steven Chang, who had learned from his girlfriend, Allison—because this was how they all stumbled upon some of the more painful truths in their lives, truths mouthed like verbal chain letters—that Darcy and her friends had been to Amy's house right before Michael showed up.

It was a sticky Saturday afternoon, and the pool, as always on weekends, was crowded. Steven and Allison were there with a group of friends, but Darcy had not come to the pool since the night she had broken up with Michael. As he was punching quarters into the soda machine during his break, Michael saw Steven coming toward him.

"Allison told me what happened," he said.

A can of root beer thumped into the tray. Michael popped open the metal tab. "Yeah? And what's that?"

"I mean about you and Darcy breaking up."

Michael merely nodded and took a sip of the soda. "It happens," he said, because he did not want to talk about Darcy.

Steven dropped a few coins into the machine and lifted a can of soda from the tray. "It was rotten what they did, though."

Michael stood perfectly still. He was afraid that if he said the wrong thing, he might never learn the truth. He stared into Steven's dark eyes. Steven's lips parted slowly.

"Oh, man, you didn't know, did you?" He flung his hands outward, sending a stream of ginger ale onto the pavement. "I thought you knew." He turned to go. "Allison's going to kill me."

Michael grabbed Steven by the arm. "Tell me," he said, tightening his grip, "what they did."

"Mike," Steven pleaded, "drop it, okay?"

Michael kept his hand clamped on Steven's arm. "This has to do with Amy, doesn't it?"

Steven turned to look at Allison and their friends, sitting on the other side of the pool. "I can't figure it out," he said. "You had Darcy. What were you doing messing around with Amy Ruggerio?"

Michael spun Steven around so fast, he almost fell over. "There is nothing going on between me and Amy. Nothing. She's a friend." He dropped his hand from Steven's arm. "I can't believe this."

"I guess Darcy thought she was something else," Steven said.

"Are you going to tell me what she did, or should I go ask Allison?"

Steven shook his head. "Hey, man, don't get pissed at me. I wasn't in on any of this."

Michael emptied his can of soda and tossed it in the recycling bin by the machine. "I'm waiting," he said.

Steven took a deep breath. "They told Amy they'd found out you and the other guys on the track team had this bet going. They said you'd bragged about how you could screw around with her mind enough so that she'd do anything for you, including sleep with every guy on the team if you asked her to. They told her each person on the team put up twenty bucks saying you couldn't do it."

Michael stared at his friend in disbelief. "They told Amy this?"

Steven nodded.

"Why?"

"Man, are you dense," Steven said. "Why do you think? To get even."

"Get even for what? I didn't do anything."

"Darcy thinks you did. She thinks you were getting some on the side from Amy the whole time you were going out with her."

Michael felt an anger so intense it frightened him. His hands clamped into fists. "I've got to get back," he told Steven, because there was nothing else left to say.

But as he swung around, his shoulder bumped against a girl who was approaching the soda machine, almost knocking her over. Michael grabbed her arm to keep her from falling. "Sorry," he mumbled, not really paying attention.

"It's okay," she told him.

Another girl stood nearby, giggling. She was extremely tall and thin with dark curly hair. Michael stared at her for a moment, trying to grasp what was happening. He had seen this girl before. She was a friend of Jenna Ward. And he knew, without even turning around to look, that the person he had almost knocked off balance was Jenna herself.

jenna

13

It had been the driest summer on record, so when the heavy rains came in mid-August, everyone said it was a blessing. People were tired of rationing water. It rained for four days straight, a pelting, pounding rain that swelled the streams and rivers, flooding backyards and carrying away lawn furniture in the dead of night. Meteorologists shrugged. They couldn't explain it either.

Jenna lay in bed, stretching lazily, still not ready to get up, and stared up at the water stain in the corner of her room. She hated the very sight of it. It had been caused by the same leak her father had been patching the day he died. She had painted over it twice, but the stain continued to bleed through the white paint. Sometimes its blurred rust-colored outline actually seemed to be creeping slowly toward her from the corner of the room. And each morning she swore the stain had grown by at least an inch or two, although she knew this was impossible.

She glanced over at the window. Tiny rivers of rain streamed down the pane of glass. Four days of this was just too much. The first rainy day, she and Andrea had hung out at the mall with their friends. It had been fun. But by the third day they had all grown bored with the routine and with each other.

She finally dragged herself out of bed, pulled on a pair of shorts and a T-shirt, ran a comb through her hair, and headed downstairs.

She was standing in the kitchen a few minutes later, buttering an English muffin, when Andrea called.

"So what's it going to be? The mall again? Or should we just rent some good movies and pig out on junk food?"

"Neither." Jenna stared out the window at the rain. She felt edgy. Maybe the weather was getting to her. "Let's do something different."

"Like?"

"I don't know. Let's just get on a bus and go somewhere."

"A bus? You're kidding. Where would we go?"

"Anywhere," she said. "It doesn't matter. The shore."

Never in a million years had she really thought they'd do it, but two different buses and two hours later, Jenna and Andrea were walking along the beach in Spring Lake.

The rain had dwindled to a mist that clung to their hair and dampened their clothes. Andrea wasn't exactly being a good sport about the whole thing.

"We could have done this on a sunny day, you know," she informed Jenna, brushing wet sand from her legs, a futile effort under the circumstances. "Think about it. You go to the beach to get a tan. To meet guys. You don't go to get your skin shriveled up from being in the rain too long." She stuck her foot in the water, rinsed the sand from it, and held it up. "My toes look like raisins."

"So walk in the sand," Jenna told her.

"It won't make any difference. It's just as wet." She stared down at her tanned toes. "They're turning white. See? They'll probably all rot and drop off."

Jenna let Andrea ramble on, for the most part ignoring her. She was used to Andrea's melodramatics.

The cold, gritty foam bit at Jenna's bare ankles as the girls walked along the water's edge. She had no idea why she had wanted to come to this place, but it felt right. She wondered if it had something to do with missing out on Nantucket this August. Every summer, for as long as she could remember, her parents had rented a cottage on the island. But her mother had decided to cancel the trip this year, explaining that she would find it too difficult.

Jenna thought she understood. Even now, feeling the wet sand ooze between her toes, she was reminded of the walks along the Nantucket beach with her father. Maybe that was why she had come: to remember. Because, although six weeks had passed since his death, Jenna still could not make herself believe that he wouldn't be coming home. Some stubborn part of her continued to think her father was on one of his business trips, and all the logic in the world could not make Jenna stop holding on to this fantasy.

As she stood by the water, looking at the gray sky blending into the gray water, unable to distinguish between the two, unable to determine the horizon, she tried to imagine the sun rising again and found that she couldn't. The waves pulled at her feet, sinking them deeper into the sand until they disappeared altogether and her body seemed to be balancing precariously on her ankles.

"Andi?" She kept her eyes on the gray scene in front of her.

"Yeah?" Andrea stood next to her, making designs in the sand with her big toe.

"I have this picture in my head. You know? I'm in a courtroom, and the jury's just found this guy guilty of killing my dad. And I walk over to the table where he's sitting with his lawyer. And I look him right in the eye, and I ask him point-blank if he knows what he's done. If he knows he destroyed three lives that day. Not just my dad's, but my mom's and mine. Because that's what he did. He killed all of us. I want him to know that. And when I can tell I'm finally getting through to him, well . . . I'm going to pull this gun out from under my sweater, and I'm going to shoot him, right there in front of the whole courtroom."

"Oh, God, Jen. You don't mean that."

"Yes. I do. And you can leave God out of it. We're not exactly on speaking terms right now."

"This isn't like you at all."

Jenna turned to look at Andrea. "What's that supposed to mean? Oh, Andi. Do you really think I'm still the same person I was six weeks ago?"

"You're scaring me." Andrea had backed away from the edge of the water. She stood with her shoulders hunched. Her arms hung at her sides defenselessly.

"I'm not deranged, Andi. Okay? Just angry." She stared down at her footless legs. "And sad. Oh, I wish you could know how sad. But you can't. No one can."

Andrea took a cautious step back into the waves, as if testing the water. Then she put her arms around her friend. "I wish I could know, too," she told her.

I t was late afternoon and raining harder than ever when they got back to Briarwood.

"I can't stand these wet clothes another minute," Andrea said, passing up Jenna's offer of a soda and heading straight for the path between their houses. "I'm outta here."

Jenna climbed the front porch steps, retrieved the mail, glanced through it for any interesting magazines, and was about to toss it all on the dining room table when she noticed an envelope addressed to her. There was no return address, but when she opened it she was amazed to find herself staring down at a letter from Amy Ruggerio.

It had been over three weeks since the incident in the theater rest room. Jenna couldn't imagine why Amy Ruggerio, of all people, would be writing to her. And so with intense curiosity she sat down on a dining room chair, forgetting all about her wet clothes, and began to read.

> *Dear Jenna,*
>
> *I'm the person who was with you in the rest room a few weeks ago when you weren't feeling well. We never introduced ourselves, but I knew who you were from your picture in the newspaper. I wanted to tell you how sorry I was about what happened to your dad, but it didn't seem like the best time. So I thought I'd write you a letter instead.*
>
> *I just wanted you to know that I understand what you're going through. I lost my dad a few years ago, too. Not just my dad, but my mom. They were in a car accident. I was seven when it happened, but it could have been yesterday; the pictures in my mind are that vivid.*
>
> *I remember how angry I was. So angry I didn't talk to anyone for almost a year. For weeks I didn't even*

let myself cry, because that would be admitting my mom and dad weren't going to come back. I think I honestly believed that as long as I didn't cry, they'd come tiptoeing into my bedroom one night, tuck me in like always, and tell me I'd been having a bad dream. But the nightmare never went away.

Then this one day I was playing at my grand-father's desk, pretending I was his secretary, and I started rummaging through the desk drawers looking for an envelope for a letter I'd written for him, and there was this plaster cast of my hand that I'd made for my mom in kindergarten. I'd painted it bright pink. I still don't know how it got there. Maybe my grandfather was saving it for me or something. Anyway when I turned it over, I saw my mom had taped a little strip of paper on the back. She'd written: "Amy's hand, age 5. I _love_ this child more than life itself." I don't know why she wrote that on there, of all places. But I'm glad she did. Because it was as if she was sending me this message, you know? I think that was the first time I re-alized she really wasn't coming home. And I just put my head down on that desk and sobbed my heart out.

It must seem like I'm rambling on here. I'm sorry. But I just wanted to share this with you, because you seem like such a nice person, and I thought it might help to know you weren't alone. If there's ever anything you need, or if you want to talk, just remember I'm here, okay?

Yours truly,
Amy Ruggerio

Jenna blinked, then stared up at the lighting fixture that hung over the dining room table. She had no idea what to think of Amy's letter. They hardly knew each other.

She read the letter again, and then a third time, trying to understand. And when she began to read it a fourth time—because now she couldn't seem to make herself *stop* reading it—she noticed that wet spots were blurring the words on the paper. It took her a moment to realize these were tears. Her tears. The first real tears she had been able to cry since her father had died. And there was nothing she could do but put her head down on the table and let them come.

14

That night Jenna's dream took on a strange new dimension. She still struggled with the tangled vines, still fought like a crazed tiger to keep from being sucked deeper into the forest, but this time, just as she had begun to gnaw through one of the vines with her teeth, she felt someone's hands—strong, competent hands—on her shoulders. When she turned around, she found herself staring right into the face of Amy Ruggerio.

She was so startled, she almost forgot that the vines were still dragging her where she didn't want to go. Then Amy cupped her hand around Jenna's elbow, and as she did, the vines fell away from Jenna's legs and waist. Now she really was moving forward. Amy was guiding her right toward the Ghost Tree, and Jenna wasn't doing anything to stop her.

She might have gone all the way into the forest if a loud thump on the roof hadn't awakened her. Sitting up in bed, head cocked, ears poised, trying to identify the sound, Jenna waited. She thought she heard a light scuffing sound, but she couldn't be certain. It was still pouring outside. She wondered if the sudden thud had been a broken branch landing on the roof, the scuffing sound only a squirrel or a raccoon.

She scrunched down between the sheets, staring up at the ceiling, as if she expected whatever was up there to come crashing through the plaster at any moment. But when the sound did not come again, she fell right back into her dream.

The mist was so thick the next morning that for a moment Jenna thought she was still trapped in the dream. She stood on the deck, holding a mug of hot tea, and squinted into the fog. Tiny beads of moisture clung to the fine hairs on her arms.

At least it had stopped raining, although there was still no sign of sunlight. It didn't matter, though. Andrea would still want to go to the pool.

Jenna sat down on the top step and leaned against the railing. She could not stop thinking about Amy Ruggerio. And she really had tried; Amy was not the type of person you thought about for any length of time, or so she believed. But Amy's sudden appearance in Jenna's dream disturbed her.

She wondered what her friends would say if they knew about Amy's letter. Probably make a big joke about it. She hated to admit it, but the whole time Amy was being so kind to her in the rest room that night, Jenna had been silently praying that no one she knew would come through the door. Thinking about that now, she felt a deep shame, not just for herself but for the way things were. It was all part of the code. No one would even dare change the rules. If they so much as tried, they'd find themselves on the outside, alone. Like Amy Ruggerio. And that was the last place Jenna wanted to be right now.

She took a sip of tea, and when she looked over the rim of

the mug, she thought she saw someone standing at the end of her yard near the path that led into the woods. But as she squinted into the mist the shadowy form darted deeper into the brush. She was trying to convince herself that she was seeing things, that her stupid dreams were finally getting to her, when a voice said, "Who was that, I wonder?"

Jenna looked up to find her mother leaning against the doorjamb, eating an orange. She was already dressed for work, although Jenna suspected it wasn't even seven o'clock yet. So her mother had seen the person, too.

Jenna shook her head. "I don't know."

Her mother stepped out on the deck and leaned against the railing. "It looked like a boy, didn't it? A teenager."

Jenna thought about this for a minute. The person appeared to be wearing cutoffs and a T-shirt and had short dark hair, but that didn't necessarily mean it was a boy. In fact, with that description it could have been Andrea, although Jenna knew it wasn't. "I'm not sure," she said finally.

Her mother went back into the kitchen and returned with a mug of steaming coffee. She ran her hand over the cushion on the lounge chair. Finding it damp, she chose to lean against the railing again.

"Maybe I shouldn't tell you this," she said, picking her words carefully. "I wouldn't want you to worry. But something strange is going on around here."

Jenna frowned. "Around here? Around our house?"

Meredith Ward took a deep breath and set her coffee mug on the railing. "Come on. You have to see this for yourself."

Jenna followed her mother upstairs to Jenna's bedroom and watched as she opened one of the windows that overlooked the front porch. Then Meredith slid the screen up, hiked up her skirt, kicked off her high heels, and started to climb out onto the roof. But with only one knee poised on the sill, she stopped. She seemed unable to move.

Jenna stared at her mother. "Are you okay?"

Meredith shook her head. "Sorry, I can't seem to bring myself to go out there. The roof, it . . . ."

"It's okay, Mom. Just tell me, then."

Her mother backed her way over to Jenna's bed and sat down. "Go look at the gutters."

Jenna peered out the window. "Okay, I'm looking. Now what?"

"Well, what do you think?"

"About what?"

"They're clean, for heaven's sake. Someone cleaned out the gutters. They've been clogged for weeks. We had a regular waterfall gushing off the roof the other day."

Jenna wondered when someone could have gotten on the roof without either her or her mother hearing anything. But then, neither of them was home much during the day. That was probably when it had happened. "Maybe it was Mr. Krebs."

"I don't think so. He's a little old to be climbing ladders and cleaning gutters."

Jenna thought of the sounds that had awakened her the night before and told her mother.

Meredith merely nodded. "I heard something, too."

"You think this person did it last night?"

Her mother shrugged. "It certainly looks that way."

Jenna felt a tingling along her spine. "Maybe it seemed like a nice thing to do, but why did this person have to go sneaking around at night?"

Her mother began to pull at a loose thread on the hem of her skirt. "There's something else."

Jenna sat down in her desk chair. She wasn't at all sure she wanted to hear more.

"Someone's been weeding the flower beds."

"This is just too weird." Jenna glanced over at the window as if she expected to catch the culprit still out on the roof.

"*Disturbing* is more like it." Her mother was trying to break the loose thread she'd been working at, but it only grew longer. "I don't care how thoughtful this person thinks he or she is being. The truth is, it makes me feel vulnerable. Especially after what happened to Charlie."

Jenna tried to shake off her own growing uneasiness. It was bad enough that a bullet could suddenly drop from the sky and change your whole life. Now she had to worry about strangers sneaking around her house at night. Wasn't there anyplace left where she could feel safe?

"I suppose I should notify the police," her mother said, crossing the room and picking up her shoes. "Let them know we have a prowler, or trespasser, or whatever, around here." She gave one last tug at the loose thread that had been annoying her. "Oh, now look what I've done."

The hem of Meredith's skirt was sagging in the front. She glanced at her watch. "Thank goodness I still have time to change." She slipped her shoes back on and headed out the door, leaving Jenna to wonder about this latest unsettling turn of events.

Judd Passarello's party was all anyone talked about at the pool during the third week of August. With school looming only two weeks away, everyone suspected this would be the last big party of the summer. Groups of friends would still get together at each other's houses. The parties would not cease completely. But the truly awesome parties, the memories of which sustained them through the school year, were coming to an end.

"My parents are best friends with the Passarellos. Judd and I practically grew up together," Andrea said one afternoon while they were at the mall buying school clothes. She had been trying all afternoon to convince Jenna to go to the party with her.

But Jenna was skeptical. "Then how come I never hear you talk about him?"

They had stopped at the cosmetics department of Macy's, and Andrea was brushing a light coating of blush on her hand to test the color. "Well, it's not like I hang out with him or his friends or anything."

"That's my point." Jenna still wasn't sure she could handle parties yet, and she was looking for any excuse she could find.

"What?" Andrea looked indignant. "We still know each other. Our families are friends. He's not going to turn us away at the front door, if that's what you're worried about." She held out the hand with the blush on it. "What do you think? Too much rose?"

"There won't be anyone there we know," Jenna argued. "It'll be mostly juniors and seniors." Then she added, "Too much rose."

Andrea wiped the blush from her hand and tried another color. "Sure there will. Everybody's heard about this party. You think nobody's going to try to crash it?" She shook her head. "I bet half the school shows up."

They wandered over to a display of perfumes. Andrea sniffed at one bottle without spraying. "Mmm . . . smell."

Jenna lifted the bottle to her nose, then sprayed a small amount on her wrist. "Half the school, including Michael Mac-Kenzie." She smiled over at Andrea.

Andrea pretended to be reading labels on the other bottles. Then she said matter-of-factly, "I heard he and Darcy Kelly broke up." She picked up another bottle, sprayed the perfume into the air, then stepped under the mist. "I just want to meet him, Jen. Is that so bad?"

A familiar uneasiness settled along Jenna's spine, as it did whenever Michael's name came up these days, although she had never mentioned this to Andrea. She told herself that the apprehension came from watching Michael—and she was now *convinced* that it was Michael—sit on the church steps across from her house almost every evening. His behavior was a little weird, maybe. But that didn't seem to be reason enough to alarm Andrea.

Jenna also knew how much it meant to Andrea to be at the same party as Michael. She was right; it *was* a chance to meet him. Maybe even talk to him. So far Andrea hadn't been very successful at the pool.

"Well?" Andrea was leaning toward her, staring her right in the face. "Hel-*lo*," she called. "You still in there?"

Jenna knew that Andrea could just as easily go to the party with any of their other friends. But she was counting on Jenna for moral support. That was what best friends were for, to help each other over the rough spots. Jenna let out an exaggerated sigh. "I know you. You won't give up until I say I'll go."

Andrea nodded agreeably. "Doesn't that make it easier?"

As they turned away from the perfume counter Jenna spotted Amy Ruggerio over by the Clinique display, trying on lipsticks. Amy smiled and waved. Jenna returned the wave, suddenly remembering Amy's letter. She wondered if Amy had expected her to write back.

"Isn't that Amy Ruggerio?" Andrea asked, looking curious.

"Yes."

"You *know* her?" Andrea's eyes widened.

"Not very well," Jenna said. But she thought perhaps she was beginning to.

15

Judd Passarello's house was on the other side of town. Andrea had talked her father, who was driving them to the party, into dropping them off two blocks away because having your father drive you to the biggest party of the summer was totally uncool.

The sound of heavy metal rumbled across the yard as Jenna and Andrea came up the front walk. Cars were everywhere. They lined both sides of the street and, having long since filled the driveway, spilled over onto the front yard. Kids were outside sitting on car hoods, some smoking, some talking, and a few making out, although most of that was going on inside the cars.

Inside the Passarellos' ranch house, bodies were wedged so tightly that Jenna wasn't sure they'd even make it through the front door. She had a childish urge to grab Andrea's hand so they wouldn't get separated.

Andrea was standing on tiptoe, squinting and trying to see over people's heads through the haze of smoke that hung over the room.

"I don't see him," she shouted over the thundering music.

Jenna knew she was talking about Michael. "So now what?" she shouted back.

"Let's find the drinks," Andrea said. "I'm thirsty."

In the kitchen they found a large laundry tub filled with ice and cans of soda. Jenna was bending over the tub when she felt someone's warm breath on her neck. She was so surprised to find Jason Friedman standing behind her that she dropped a can of soda on his foot.

Jason winced, then picked up the can and set it on top of the refrigerator. "I wouldn't try to open that right now," he said. "Unless you want to spend the rest of the evening cleaning the Passarellos' ceiling."

Jenna was sure her pulse rate had reached two hundred. She took a step back and leaned against the counter for support. Ever since the night she had had the panic attack in the movie theater, she had managed to keep Jason at a distance. She went out with him sometimes, but only when she knew they would be with their other friends. The rest of the time she made up what she hoped were plausible excuses.

Jason pulled two cans of soda from the tub and handed her one. She took it, praying that he wouldn't notice she was shaking.

"I was hoping you'd be here." Jason seemed almost shy around her, which only made her feel more awkward. "Want to go outside? The smoke in here is really bothering my eyes."

Without actually answering him, Jenna slipped out the sliding glass door that led to a deck. Jason followed. The deck was as crowded as the rest of the house. Jenna began to walk toward the front yard, although she had no idea where she was going, or why.

There was no place to sit on the front steps, so they made

their way to one of the cars on the lawn and sat on the hood. Jenna tried to open her soda, but her hands were shaking so badly she couldn't grab the metal tab. So she closed her eyes and concentrated on her breathing. Gradually the anxiety began to subside. When she opened her eyes, it was to find Jason staring at her, a worried look on his face.

He took the can from her and pulled open the tab. "Are you okay?"

"Yes," she lied.

After an unbearably awkward silence Jason said, "You know, I've been calling you almost every day and leaving messages on your answering machine."

Jenna was struggling to think clearly and was still concentrating hard on her breathing.

"You never call back." Jason stared down at his can of soda.

"I'm sorry. It's just that . . ." What could she say? She couldn't tell him how anxious he made her feel. He'd want to know why. And she didn't have an answer for that.

Jason raised his hand as if he were a witness being sworn in. "Never mind. Forget it."

"I guess I thought I'd see you at the pool, so I didn't bother. Calling back, I mean," Jenna said. But she suddenly remembered that she hadn't seen him at the pool for over a week and that, in a way, she had felt relieved.

Jason shook his head. "I've been working on my science project. I haven't had much time for the pool." He was looking straight at her. "Or maybe you didn't notice."

A flood of mixed emotions welled up in her. "I noticed," she whispered.

He took a deep breath, then swallowed. "Man, this is hard."

"What?"

"Telling you what I'm thinking."

"I thought you could tell me just about anything," Jenna said, remembering how they had talked for hours at other parties and on the phone.

"This is different." He rolled his can of soda back and forth between his palms.

"Why?"

"Because it's about us."

Jenna had just managed to calm down; now her heart began to thump all over again. "What about us?"

"That's the thing," he said. "*Is* there an us?"

Jenna forced herself to look into his eyes. His beautiful, soft gray eyes. Was it true? Did she really feel nothing for him anymore? She wondered what he would say if she told him about the awful effect he'd been having on her. After all, wasn't it kinder than leaving him in the dark? And she might have done just that, told him everything, if Andrea hadn't suddenly come running across the yard, navigating gracefully between cars.

"There you are!" she shrieked. "I've been looking everywhere for you." She hopped up on the hood of the car next to Jenna. Her face glowed bright pink. "He's here," she announced.

"Where?" Jenna knew full well she was talking about Michael MacKenzie.

"Okay . . ." Andrea's breath was coming in short, excited bursts. "Okay, now don't look. Promise me you won't look. Or he'll know."

Jenna was aware that Jason was frowning at both of them. She had no idea what was going through his mind, but she secretly prayed he wouldn't think this had anything to do with her recent behavior toward him. "Fine," she said, "we won't look."

"He's right across the street in that gray Honda." Andrea made short, jerky motions with her hands. "Don't look. Don't look."

"We're not," Jenna said. "Calm down."

Jason was staring across the street. "Isn't that one of the lifeguards from the pool?"

"Yes," Andrea answered, almost breathless.

Jason looked over at Jenna. Then he slid off the car. "I think I get the picture," he said, clenching and unclenching his fists as he headed back toward the house.

As the screen door banged behind Jason it was all Jenna could do not to run after him. Instead she told herself that maybe it was better to let him think what he wanted. It meant she wouldn't have to explain anything to him. It was easier this way.

"What's his problem?" Andrea asked.

Jenna answered with a silent shrug.

Andrea grabbed Jenna's arm. "Michael's not with anyone. He's just been sitting there for who knows how long. Why do you think he isn't coming inside? Do you think he's waiting for someone? Do you—"

Jenna made a time-out sign with her hands. "Whoa, slow down."

Andrea puffed out her cheeks and covered her eyes with her hand. "I'm acting like a complete idiot. Sorry."

"No, you're not," Jenna assured her.

"It's just that I've built this whole thing up in my mind, you know? And here he is, sitting right over there. And my heart feels like it's going to fly right out of my chest." She looked over at Jenna. "I can't seem to stop shaking. Isn't that the stupidest thing?"

Jenna glanced across the lawn at the gray Honda and was surprised to find Michael watching her. Goose bumps ran along her arms. Michael's eyes suddenly widened, as if he had just realized she was looking at him, too. But he turned away before she could be sure.

"Why don't you go over and talk to him?" Jenna suggested.

"You're kidding. Just waltz up there and introduce my-self?"

Jenna noticed Michael was now leaning forward. He had his arms folded on top of the steering wheel, his forehead pressed against his hand. She was reminded of the evenings she had watched him on the front steps of the church, knees pulled up to his chest, head bent. She had felt his pain then, and she felt it now. She wished there were some way to offer him comfort.

"Why not?" she said, her voice barely above a whisper. "He looks like he could use a friend."

"Fine. *You* talk to him."

"Maybe I will." She stood up, surprising even herself, and marched right over to the Honda. After all, Andrea couldn't go on like this forever. Somebody had to put her out of her misery. It might as well be her best friend.

And the truth was, Jenna herself was a little curious about Michael. She wanted to know why he sat on the church steps across from her house almost every evening. Not that she'd come right out and ask him. Still, if Michael and Andrea became friends, then maybe someday Jenna would have an answer to that question.

But as Jenna approached the car, she heard the engine

roar to life. She had the feeling Michael MacKenzie would have torn right out of his parking space, leaving only the smell of burning rubber in the air, if she hadn't already rested her hand on the edge of the open window. She tried to smile reassuringly, although she wasn't sure why she needed to.

"You'll probably think this is really dumb," she said, "but my friend over there has been wanting to meet you." She nodded in Andrea's direction. Andrea stood stock-still, as if she were a rabbit facing a hungry wolf.

Michael glanced over his shoulder to where Jenna had nodded. "I'd like to meet your friend," he said. "But not tonight, okay?" His voice was thick, slow, as if he were weighing each word. "I have to leave right now. I'm meeting someone."

Jenna smiled at him. It was a mechanical smile, but she didn't dare show her disappointment. "Maybe at the next party." She backed away from the car so that he could pull out.

When she risked turning around, she saw that Andrea was no longer in sight. But standing on the front steps of the Passarellos' house, watching her intently, watching the entire scene between her and Michael MacKenzie, was Amy Ruggerio.

few minutes later, when Jenna went back to the party to look for Andrea, she spotted Amy in the corner of the dining room trying to get rid of some guy. There was something about the boy that gave Jenna the creeps. He was wearing a rolled-up blue bandanna around his head and had an earring in the shape of a skull dangling from one ear. But it wasn't the way he dressed that bothered her. Lots of kids dressed like he did. No, it was something else, something in his behavior, and the way he kept trying to force himself on Amy.

For a split second she considered going up to Amy and pretending she wanted to talk to her, just to get this guy off her back. But then she thought better of it. It really wasn't any of her business. When she came back through the dining room again a few minutes later, she saw Amy escaping alone out the back door, and she felt an unexpected relief.

She finally found Andrea sitting under a tree in the Passarellos' backyard. Her eyes were wet and red-rimmed. And the first thing she did when she saw Jenna was yank a fistful of grass from the lawn and throw it at her.

"I can't believe you did that!" she shrieked.

Jenna kept a safe distance from her. There was no telling what else Andrea might decide to throw. "Come on, Andi. You wanted to meet him, didn't you?"

A small rock whizzed by, only inches from Jenna's head.

"I've never been so embarrassed in my life." Andrea kept feeling the space around her with her hands, trying to find another rock to throw.

"Sure you have," Jenna reminded her cheerfully. "Remember fifth grade, in music, when Miss Cobb tapped you on the head with the ruler, which meant everybody else stopped singing and you had to sing solo? And she kept making you sing it over and over again, smacking that dumb ruler on your desk to keep the beat, because you couldn't get the notes right?"

"Thank you for reminding me of that."

Another rock whipped by, just missing Jenna's shoulder.

"Look, in the ultimate scheme of things, just how important can this be?" Jenna risked taking a few steps forward, then sat down beside Andrea. "I mean, it's not like this is life-threatening. It's not like I tried to talk him into taking you out or anything."

"The ultimate scheme of things?" Andrea's mouth hung open.

Jenna pointed to the stars that had formed a thick canopy overhead. "You know. The grand design. Or whatever." She grinned at Andrea good-naturedly. "Sort of puts things in perspective, doesn't it?"

Andrea punched her in the shoulder. "Michael MacKenzie, for your information, just happens to be part of my *own* grand design. Or was, until tonight, anyway."

"I'm sorry, Andi. I was just trying to help."

"I know you were." Andrea took the sleeve of her shirt and wiped her eyes. Sooty spots of mascara stained the material, but she didn't seem to notice. "It's okay. I mean, you didn't even want to come to this party in the first place, and—"

"I just didn't think I was ready, that's all. It's a little soon. It's hard to be around people who are having a great time when you feel so empty inside."

Andrea nodded and sniffed. "And you came anyway. For me." She rested her head on Jenna's shoulder. "It doesn't matter about Michael."

After a few minutes of silence Jenna said, "All I did was tell him you wanted to meet him. And he said he'd like to meet you, too. Only he couldn't right then because he had to leave."

"He said that? He said he wanted to meet me?" Andrea brushed the smudgy wet spots from her cheeks, looking hopeful.

"Yes. He said, 'I'd like to meet your friend.' That's exactly what he said. His exact words."

Andrea seized Jenna's arm. "You mean that? You're not making it up?"

"Why would I make it up?" Jenna shook her head. "Next party. You'll see."

Andrea leaned back against the tree, closed her eyes, and sighed. "Next party," she whispered.

It took five difficult math problems before Jenna felt calm enough to go to bed. The whole night had been an emotional roller-coaster ride. First Jason, then Andrea, even Amy. Then there was the odd feeling she had had when she saw Michael MacKenzie watching her from his car. She had begun to wonder if his sitting on those church steps almost every evening had something to do with her.

Jenna erased the proof to the second equation. It was all wrong. She brushed off her paper and stared down at the problem, but the numbers blurred on the page. A larger puzzle filled her mind. Was it possible Michael was interested in her? She shook her head, immediately dismissing the idea. She felt disloyal to Andrea for even thinking such a thing.

Besides, he wouldn't have been in such an all-fired hurry to drive off if that were the case. And who was she kidding? She might be okay to look at, but Andrea was downright gorgeous.

Jenna bent over the last math problem on the page. If only relationships could be worked out through mathematics. But that was impossible. There were simply too many variables.

She'd probably never figure these people out. Not Andrea, or Michael, or Amy, or Jason. It was all so complicated.

Exhausted, Jenna closed her math book, slipped on her nightgown, and crawled into bed, hoping to go right to sleep. Instead she lay awake for hours, trying to decide what to do about Jason.

And when she did fall asleep, her dreams gave her little

peace. Because this time, as she stumbled through the dark forest with Amy beside her, another person appeared. Jenna was almost halfway down the path when she spotted a boy up ahead, sitting beneath the Ghost Tree. And even with his head down, his arms folded about his bent knees, she knew it was Michael MacKenzie.

michael

16

It was almost Labor Day weekend, and Michael had begun to breathe easier. Maybe Joe had been right. The police just didn't have enough evidence to put together a case. He knew from general neighborhood gossip, usually shared by his mother over dinner, that Healey and Boyle had finally finished questioning everyone in the area. The process had taken a lot longer than expected because many of the families had been on vacation. But no one had come back to his house or asked any more questions. So Michael dared to hope.

With school less than a week away, he had gone back to his daily routine of running, trying to get in shape for track. He had done very little training since early July. But now he ran almost every morning at dawn and again in the early evening, to make up for lost time.

On most nights, after he'd run several miles, he would end up resting on the church steps across from Jenna's house, just as he had been doing since the accident. But he had grown increasingly uneasy about these visits ever since she had approached him two nights ago at Judd's party. He could not remember a single word of that conversation with Jenna. He remembered only glancing in the rearview mirror as he maneuvered out of his parking space, and catching a glimpse of her face, frozen in the pale glow of the streetlight. It was obvious that she knew who he was. She probably recognized him from the pool. She was bound to wonder what he was doing hanging out across from her house.

He had not wanted to stop by Judd Passarello's party that night. He'd known Darcy would probably be there. So far the two of them had managed to avoid each other since they had broken up. Darcy stayed within the secure confines of her group of friends whenever she came to the pool, and Michael had not been to a single party since Steven Chang's. That is, he had not actually set foot inside any of the houses where the parties were under way. Instead, much to his dismay, he found himself waiting outside these houses in his father's car, hoping to get a glimpse of Amy.

He had tried calling her on several occasions, but she had never returned his calls. He even wrote her letters explaining everything, about how Darcy had just been trying to get back at him. The letters came back, unopened. His sense of loss was far greater than he had ever imagined it would be. For the first time in his life, he felt absolutely alone in the world.

He stared across the road at Jenna's house. The yard was looking pretty good these days. He was proud of that. For weeks the flower beds had gone untended. The Wards did have a local boy mow the lawn each week, but the flower beds had disturbed Michael. They'd been choked with weeds. He wondered what Charlie Ward would have thought if he could have seen them.

And so Michael had taken to weeding the flower beds each night after Jenna and her mother had gone to sleep. He had more or less appointed himself the Wards' personal caretaker. He thought Charlie Ward would approve.

When the heavy rains had come in mid-August, Michael had noticed how the water flowed off the roof instead of coming down the drainpipe. The water formed large pools around the foundation. If their basement wasn't already flooded, it soon would be. So he had come up with a plan.

He had waited until almost four in the morning to leave his own house. When he got to the Wards', he sneaked into the garage, found an extension ladder, and as quietly as possible climbed up on the roof. The soles of his sneakers had almost no traction on the wet rungs, so he kicked off his shoes and mounted the ladder barefoot. Two large plastic trash bags bulged from his back pockets.

Using his hands, he dug at the clumps of wet leaves and twigs, tossing them into the bags. The heavy rain blinded him, making it difficult to see what he was doing and slowing him down. Unlike those other times when he came to weed the flower beds, he had badly underestimated the time it would take to clean the gutters. He had suddenly realized it was almost daybreak. Fearing discovery, he had retrieved his sneakers, carried the ladder back to the garage, then dragged the trash bags out to the woods at the back of the house to dump the soggy contents. He had forgotten his watch, and the thick mist had tricked him into thinking it was earlier than it really was. So the last thing he expected to see as he came out of the woods was Jenna sitting on the steps of the deck, staring right in his direction.

Momentarily stunned, he had wadded the empty trash bags in his hands and darted back into the woods, avoiding the path. He stopped a few yards away, crouched behind a clump of shrubs, and watched as Mrs. Ward came out onto the deck and began talking to Jenna. Neither of them seemed alarmed about anything, least of all a trespasser. He had let himself breathe again. Maybe she hadn't seen him after all.

But now he wasn't so sure, because on this particular evening he saw a patrol car drive by twice. It was obvious that the officer was paying particular attention to the Ward house. When the police car came by a third time, Michael recognized the Hangman behind the wheel. He was no longer watching the Ward house. His attention was on Michael. As the car slowed down, Michael got to his feet. It took tremendous effort, but he managed a friendly smile and a wave as he jogged down the church steps and headed nowhere in particular, glancing over his shoulder occasionally to make sure he wasn't being followed.

It was only six o'clock. So he began to run again, and he would have kept on running until he collapsed if he hadn't seen Amy Ruggerio getting into her grandfather's car in front of the local 7-Eleven. He stopped so abruptly he almost fell over.

Amy was obviously flustered by his sudden appearance. Her hand rested nervously on her throat. Caught off guard, she seemed less defensive than the last time he had tried to talk to her. He approached her cautiously, as if he were afraid she might vanish into thin air if he made one false move.

They were standing less than three feet apart. Michael glanced into the car to see if anyone was with her. She was alone.

Neither of them spoke. Then, just as the awkward silence threatened to blow Michael apart, Amy said, "I had to get some eggs. We were out."

It was as if they were picking up in the middle of a conversation, right where they'd left off. Eggs, for pete's sake! Michael wanted to burst out laughing. He wanted to throw his arms around her. But he did neither. "Do you have to go right home?"

Amy glanced back at the 7-Eleven. She seemed preoccupied. "I think I'd better."

"None of what she said was true, you know. Darcy, I mean. She was trying to get back at me."

Amy's eyes glazed over with a few renegade tears. But she fought them back.

"I care too much about you to ever do anything to hurt you." He had not meant to put it all on the line like that, but somehow the words had just come out.

Amy slowly took a step back toward the car. She reached behind her and grabbed the door handle. "It isn't just about Darcy," she whispered, pulling the door open.

Michael shook his head. "Then what? Tell me what it is."

"Your party . . ."

At the mention of his party, his body tensed. "What about it?"

"I don't know." Amy's face flushed a soft pink. "I guess I've been wondering how—no, not how, *why*—we ended up in your garage."

Michael had no idea where this was leading. What could he say? That the only thing he'd had on his mind that afternoon was sex? He tried desperately to recall what he had said to her at the party. He'd fed her a line, he didn't doubt that, but what? And what had he said to her in the garage when they were rolling around on a pile of old lawn furniture cushions his mother was planning to throw away? Something about having wanted her since the first time he set eyes on her. It had been a bald-faced lie. Or so he thought. Now, standing across from her in the 7-Eleven parking lot, he wasn't so sure.

Amy was still waiting for his answer.

"I wanted you, okay?" He almost moaned the words.

"But I was with Joe." She narrowed her eyes at him. "I was his . . . date."

Michael did not miss the disdain in her voice.

"I'm just trying to understand something. About what was going on. I mean, Joe's your best friend, isn't he?" Amy rested one hand on the top of the open car door, as if for support. "Why would you try to move in on your friend's date?"

Michael spread his hands. He looked like a preacher about to deliver a benediction. "It wasn't like that."

"Then what was it like?"

"What?"

Amy sighed and stared up at the sky. "The artful dodger."

"The what?"

"You keep dodging my questions." She shook her head and slid into the front seat of her grandfather's car.

Michael was practically at his wits' end. "What about us?" he managed to say as she was inching the car out of the lot. "Can I see you again?"

Amy rolled down the window and stared up at him. Then she closed her eyes. When she opened them again, she said, "I need time, Mike. We have things we need to . . . talk about."

"We can talk now," he said, brushing her hair over her shoulder and lightly touching her face.

Amy smiled. It was just the tiniest curve of her full lips. But it was a smile. He was certain of it. "Later, okay?"

He watched her pull out of the parking lot, then took off for home. It was almost dinnertime. He felt lighter, somehow, and his feet were moving faster than ever; his body seemed to fly. Being in love could do that to you.

Fifteen minutes later Michael bounded up the front steps, through the house, and into the kitchen just in time to find Ralph Healey, Doug Boyle, and two other men from the police force scanning his backyard with metal detectors.

oug Boyle and Sergeant Healey searched along the edge of the woods behind the house, while two cops Michael didn't recognize carefully skirted the area around the large above-ground pool.

"I don't know what to tell you," Michael's mother said when he asked what was going on. "They have a search warrant." Karen MacKenzie was at the back door, watching the police comb through her yard with their equipment. "They've been all over this house. They've gone through all our . . . things." Her shoulders twitched, as if she had just told him she'd found cockroaches in the bread box.

His heart began to thump wildly. The police knew something. That was why they had come back.

He spotted his father and Josh outside, standing with their arms folded, side by side on the patio, looking as if they were prepared to defend their small two-story colonial with their lives if they had to. He tried to determine the look on his father's face, to see how much he knew, but Tom MacKenzie's face was blank, like that of a man stunned by an unexpected blow.

Michael looked over at the woodpile behind the garage.

No one was back there. But then, he seriously doubted the metal detectors would be able to locate the rifle where he'd hidden it: three feet in the ground below all that wood.

Out of the corner of his eye, he saw Doug Boyle disappear into the dense woods. He emerged a few minutes later holding something on the end of a stick. He studied it for a few minutes, then brought it to Ralph Healey. The older man called the other two officers over to look at what Boyle had found.

Michael's father glanced toward the back door. Without a word, Karen MacKenzie punched open the screen door with the side of her fist and stepped out onto the patio. Michael followed her, although each step he took felt as if his feet were weighted.

Doug Boyle handed the stick, with something stuck on the end of it, to Healey, who dropped the object into a plastic bag, sealing it as he walked toward the patio. He held it out to Michael's father. "Doug found this empty casing over in the woods there," he said.

That was when Michael realized Boyle had purposely slipped a stick inside the shell in order to pick it up. He didn't want to contaminate possible evidence.

Michael stared down at the two-inch casing as a wave of panic swept over him. Of course the empty shell would have been ejected after he fired the gun. Why hadn't he thought of that? Why hadn't he tried to find it?

"All you've got there is an empty casing," Tom MacKenzie said. "How do you know it matches the bullet?"

Healey told Boyle and the other men to meet him out front. When they'd gone, he turned back to Tom MacKenzie. "The bullet that killed Charlie Ward was a forty-five-caliber, five-hundred-grain. One of those old lead bullets the government used to issue to the cavalry." He pointed to the bottom of the cartridge, where .45-70 GOVT was printed. "You don't see too many of these around anymore. It didn't come from a pistol. Too big." He looked over at Michael. "The bullet came from a forty-five-seventy rifle, son."

Michael felt a tightness in his throat. The bullet Ralph Healey described was identical to the ones Michael's grandfather had given him along with the Winchester. At the time, his grandfather had explained that he'd had the bullets for years but that they were still good. He'd given Michael several rounds.

"Are you saying Mike fired that shot?" Karen MacKenzie asked, grabbing her husband's arm for support.

Healey stuffed the bag with the casing into his pocket, then pulled out a pack of Marlboros. He looked apologetic as he lit a cigarette. "Sorry, I haven't been able to kick the habit yet." He took a long draw on the cigarette. "I'm not saying Mike shot it," he told Karen MacKenzie. "I'm just saying it looks like it came from his rifle."

Tom MacKenzie's face had turned a deep red. Michael could see he was furious but working hard to control it. "That rifle was locked in my gun cabinet in the basement," he sputtered. "I put it there myself." He spun around and was almost nose to nose with Michael. "Do you know anything about this?"

Michael ran his tongue back and forth along his lower lip. "Well, I did take it out for a few minutes to show a couple of my friends." This part was true. What he didn't bother to mention was that he and Joe had then taken the gun back into the woods. Nor did he mention that he had left it propped next to the garage door later, while he was with Amy. "But I put it back."

"Did you lock the cabinet?" His father narrowed his eyes.

Michael puffed up his cheeks, pretending to remember. "Sure. At least, I think I did."

"You *think* you did?"

Michael could tell by the way his father was clenching his jaw that he was only seconds away from exploding.

"Dad . . . I'm sorry. I can't remember." He tried to swallow, but his mouth was too dry. "I didn't shoot that rifle, if that's what you're thinking."

Tom MacKenzie's red face paled to a neutral pink. Michael had managed to defuse him for the moment.

"Well, then, who did?" his mother asked.

Michael forced himself to look at his mother. The fear in her face was terrible to see.

"Anybody could have fired it," his father told Ralph Healey. "There were over forty people here that day."

Sergeant Healey looked at Michael, then turned to Michael's father. "Forty people?"

"It was Mike's birthday," Tom MacKenzie told him. "We threw him a big party. The rifle was one of his gifts."

"So you're saying maybe somebody decided to try it out when no one was looking?"

"Why not? Kids do crazy things these days." But even as his father said this, Michael could see the desperation on his face. He was grasping at straws.

Ralph Healey took a drag of his cigarette, then squinted through the smoke. "You were here the whole time?"

Michael's parents nodded in unison.

"And you didn't hear a rifle shot?"

"It was the Fourth of July," Michael reminded him, working hard to steady his voice. "People were setting off firecrackers and cherry bombs all over the neighborhood. Nobody would have known the difference."

Michael's father sat down on the lounge chair. "Do you have any idea who might have done something like this?" he asked Michael. "I mean, which of your friends could have sneaked off to the woods back there and fired the rifle?"

Michael shook his head. "Sorry," he said. "I didn't see anyone touch it."

Josh had remained unusually quiet amid all the questions. But now he said, "What about Joe?"

They all turned to him. Michael felt the prickle of sweat on his face. He knew where this was going.

"What *about* him?" his father asked.

"Why did he suddenly want to borrow Mike's rifle?" Josh looked incredibly pleased with himself. A thin, crooked smile spread across his face. "Then when Mike wants it back, Joe tells him it was stolen. If you ask me—"

"We're not asking you," Michael interjected angrily. "You're talking about a friend of mine." But it was too late.

Ralph Healey tossed the half-smoked cigarette on the ground and crushed it beneath his shoe. Michael could see he was giving Josh's idea serious thought, although he didn't say anything.

Michael's eyes were so dry they had begun to burn. He wondered if he had dared to blink even once since he'd come home and found half the Briarwood police force scouting his backyard. His tongue felt like an oversized cotton ball. "At least forty other people were here that day," he reminded Healey. "I know it doesn't look good for Joe, but you can't pin something on him just because of some lousy coincidence. It's not his fault the gun was stolen."

"If it *was* stolen," Josh said.

Michael fought the urge to pummel his brother into the ground.

Ralph Healey shook his head. "I'll need a list of everyone who was here that day," he said. "Maybe somebody saw or heard something."

After the police had gone, Michael went inside with his family. They all sat down at the kitchen table as if they were going to eat dinner, although there was no food on the table and no dishes had been set out.

For a while no one said anything. Michael looked up at the clock. It was past seven-thirty. His father and Josh had missed *Jeopardy!* and hadn't seemed to notice. If he had not felt so miserable, he might have found that funny.

"I bet it *was* that Sadowski kid," his father said. "This is just like something he'd do." Michael knew his father needed to believe Joe had fired the rifle, because it was too terrible to imagine it might have been one of his own sons.

"Tom, we don't know that for a fact." Karen MacKenzie reached over and pressed her hand gently on his back.

"Can we have pizza?" Josh asked. "I'll call."

His mother nodded. "Go ahead. I don't feel much like cooking."

Tom MacKenzie pulled a can of beer from the refrigerator, then leaned against the refrigerator door. He stared down at Michael. "You know anything more about this?"

"Dad, I told the police everything I know."

His father, seemingly satisfied with Michael's answer, took a long swallow of beer. Then he began to drone on about the afternoon's investigation. Michael had to force himself to listen. His mind was racing all over the place. According to his father, the police had gone through the entire house, probably looking for the Winchester, before bringing out the metal detectors and scanning the backyard. If they had come to the house looking for the rifle, Michael suddenly realized, then they had never believed it was stolen in the first place. And his parents were probably thinking the same thing, which was why his father was so desperately trying to point the finger at Joe.

All this time Michael had been living with a false hope, believing that he had gotten the cops off his back after the first round of questions three weeks ago. And all this time they had suspected him. They had known all along that the bullet was a .45-caliber, 500-grain. When their investigation turned up no other guns in the area big enough to fire a bullet that size, they had come back to the one person who did own such a gun: Michael MacKenzie.

Things had gotten far worse than he'd ever imagined. At least he had bought a little time by telling Ralph Healey he'd give him a list of the kids who were at his party. It would take a while to question all of them. Michael felt a twinge of guilt. Somehow he had managed to drag forty of his friends into the mire. But that wasn't what was making him feel sick; he knew they'd be questioned and that would be the end of it. No. What made his empty stomach turn sour was that he had done almost nothing to defend Joe. He had let Josh mouth off about his theory, raising Healey's suspicions. He could have kept the investigation from going any further. He could have pointed the police in a different direction. All he had had to do was stand up and say that he was the person they were looking for. That he was Charlie Ward's murderer. Instead he had kept silent.

Now he had no choice. He would have to tell Joe what he had done. He had to let him know what had happened before the cops showed up at Joe's house with a warrant for his arrest.

ichael lay awake most of the night wondering how to break the news to Joe. Then, while the neighbor's cat foraged below his window for crickets in the early-morning hours, Michael finally fell asleep, only to awaken a few hours later in sheets soaked with the sweat of his nightmares.

That morning he called Joe and told him to meet him in the parking lot at the pool after work. If Joe was surprised or even curious, he didn't let on, simply saying that he'd be there.

Michael had seen Joe only a few times since the day he had come by Michael's house to tell him how it had gone with the police. He wondered if Joe thought he was avoiding him, although Joe hadn't exactly been seeking him out, either. But whatever was going on between them, Michael needed to believe he could still count on his friend. And sure enough, after work he found Joe leaning against his red Mustang in the parking lot, arms folded, head tipped forward as if he were dozing. He wore a rolled-up blue bandanna tied around his head. The single skull earring danced in the late-afternoon sunlight.

"What's the deal?" he said when he saw Michael coming.

"Not here," Michael told him.

Joe eyed him intently, then shrugged. "So get in the car. We'll go wherever you want."

Michael hadn't thought about going anywhere in the car. He hadn't set foot inside the Mustang since the day he failed his first driver's test. He felt his chest tighten as Joe opened the car door. His nerves on edge, he listened as the engine roared awake, bringing the radio on full blast.

"I miss my CD player," Joe said when Michael finally managed to force himself into the passenger seat. Then he grinned. "Think the cops'll ever find the guy who stole it?" When Michael didn't respond, Joe leaned down and pulled a can of beer from underneath the driver's seat. He tugged at the metal tab, and warm beer erupted onto his hand like white lava. He chugged the entire can within seconds, crushed it beneath his foot, and tossed it under the car parked next to him. "Can't get caught with an open can in the car while I'm driving," he said, wiping his mouth with the back of his hand. "Rules are rules." Then he laughed.

Michael was painfully aware that Joe was rarely without a can of beer in his hand these days, at least on those few occasions when he'd seen him. Before, he had drunk only at parties. But this was something new. If Michael allowed himself to think about it, which he tried not to, he would have to admit that Joe's drinking had gotten worse since they had learned about Charlie Ward's death.

Joe shifted the car into reverse and backed out of the space. "So are you gonna talk, or what?"

"Just drive," Michael told him.

"Drive where?"

"Anywhere. The Swamp."

For some reason he could not explain, Michael felt drawn

to the Great Swamp that afternoon. And because it was a week-day, he knew not many people would be around.

Joe parked the car, pulled an old backpack from the trunk, filled it with three cans of beer, then headed toward the first trail. Michael followed. In the past he would have worried about being caught in the Swamp with beer. But that didn't matter much now.

He knew without asking where Joe was headed. So when they came to a bend in the trail that opened into a wide circle, he cupped a hand over his brow and stared up at the Ghost Tree as if he had just run into an old friend he hadn't seen in years.

The ground beneath the tree was completely bare. No ferns, no grass. Not even weeds grew there. And in the middle, solemn and majestic, stood the ancient and enormous syca-more. Hazy sunlight spilled down between its leaves. It looked far from ghostly.

He had heard once that the tree had gotten its name from the way it looked in the winter. Without its leaves, the thick bare branches appeared smooth and white, like brittle bones reaching skyward. Ancient souls were said to dance around the tree at midnight whenever there was a full moon. But for all the spooky old legends, the tree had never seemed haunted to him. And he and Joe had spent hundreds of hours beneath its branches.

Funny, he hadn't thought about the Ghost Tree for years, except for that time in the park when he met Joe to explain about the stolen gun story.

Joe walked around to the other side of the circle, where the path continued, and Michael followed. They had gone only a few yards when Joe stepped off the path into the woods, slapping branches out of his way. Michael knew Joe was heading for the pond, a special place they'd discovered years ago.

Their sneakers made sucking sounds in the soft mud as they walked along. The pond was only fifty yards or so from the Ghost Tree, but when they were kids it had seemed to take them hours to get there.

Within minutes they were clearing a space beneath a tree a few feet from the edge of the pond. It had been at least three years since they had last come to this spot. Joe rubbed his back against the rough bark, like a lazy bear, then slid comfortably to the ground. Michael sat beside him so that he would not have to look directly at his face.

Through the branches, he could just make out the top of the Ghost Tree. He thought about the times he and Joe had dared each other to spend the night there alone. Kids were always daring each other to sleep in the Ghost Tree. They claimed that if you could survive the night there alone, you could survive anything. It had become a kind of rite of passage for some of them, although Michael had never actually met anyone who had done it.

Joe took a beer from his backpack and offered it to Michael, who declined. "Okay, we're ten thousand miles from civilization," he said, yanking open the tab. "Now are you going to tell me what's going on?"

"The cops were at my house last night," Michael said.

"Again? Man, they never give up."

Michael kept his eyes on the pond. On the other side, a large snapping turtle was slowly, laboriously pulling itself up onto a rock. "They know the bullet came from the Winchester."

Out of the corner of his eye, he saw a stream of beer escape from Joe's mouth as he suddenly jerked the can away.

Joe grabbed his wet T-shirt, squeezing it with his hand. "*Your* Winchester? How do they know it was *your* Winchester?"

Michael told him everything that had taken place the night before. How they had traced the bullet to his gun and had found the empty casing in the woods behind the house. He told him everything except that the suspicion had shifted to Joe.

Joe finished the beer and opened another. "I keep telling you, man, they can't prove a damn thing without the rifle. If they don't have the murder weapon, they don't have a case."

Dragonflies skimmed the surface of the pond. Michael picked up a flat stone and skipped it over the water. He had never felt so lost before. Always, there was Joe. From the first time they met, even as small boys, he had known he could tell Joe anything, because Joe would not judge him. He would only listen. But that was not going to happen this time. And he knew, too, that no matter how all of this turned out, they would never come back to this place again.

"You need to know something," he said quietly.

Joe had leaned his head back against the tree and appeared to be dozing. Without opening his eyes, he said, "What's that?"

The air felt so heavy Michael thought he might drown if he took a breath. "Healey's got this idea that maybe you borrowed the rifle and then said it was stolen to cover up the fact you fired it."

Joe's silence was deafening. It beat against Michael's ears until the ache crept into his skull. When Joe finally did speak, his voice was low. The words slipped from his tongue like slow drops from a leaking faucet. "Yeah? And where would he have gotten that idea?"

Michael knew Joe was staring right at the side of his face.

He could feel his friend's warm breath against his ear, but he kept his eyes straight ahead. "Who knows how Healey's mind works?" he said. "He's desperate. He's got to make a case out of something. This thing's been going on for weeks now."

"So he's going to make me a suspect?"

Michael skipped another small rock into the pond, but it hit the water wrong and sank. He watched the ripples tear at the surface. "Maybe not. It could be a bluff. Healey wants me to give him a list of everyone who was at my party. That's forty other potential suspects to keep him busy for a while."

Joe flattened the beer can against the tree with the palm of his hand. "And what am I supposed to do in the meantime? Just sit back and wait for them to come arrest me?"

The look on his friend's face was more than Michael could bear. "No. That's not going to happen. I'll tell them the truth first."

Joe was chugging the last of the three beers. "Either way I get nailed," he said. "I'm an accessory, remember? And don't forget, I'm the one who filed the false police report." He stood up, swaying slightly, and threw the empty, crushed cans into the backpack. "Man, life really sucks, doesn't it?"

Michael pulled himself up and put his hand on his friend's shoulder. "Joe . . . what can I say, man? I never meant for any of this to happen. I don't know how everything got so screwed up."

At first Joe nodded, as if he understood, but Michael could see the twitching tightness in his jaw. It made him think of a wild animal about to bare its fangs. Then he said, "Yeah, well, screwing things up seems to be what you do best these days."

Michael could only stare back at him. "What's that supposed to mean?"

"Look at you, man. You had it all. Big jock at school, colleges practically knocking down your door . . ." His eyes narrowed. "A babe like Darcy Kelly."

Michael waited. He had no idea where this was going.

But Joe only let out a disgusted snort, then turned and began to walk back toward the car.

Michael could think of nothing to do but follow. It was a long walk back to his house, and besides, Joe was in no condition to drive.

When they reached the car, Michael asked for the keys. Surprisingly, Joe didn't argue; he merely handed them over without comment. The minute Michael put his hands on the steering wheel, they began to sweat. This was where it had all begun. Less than two months ago he had sat behind this same wheel, Joe by his side, on his way to take his driver's test. Nothing stood in the way of his future. Nothing, until a stranger's voice, floating over the airwaves from fifty miles away, had told him he had killed a man.

Joe was slumped down in the seat. His head bounced loosely against the headrest. Michael wondered if Joe had fallen asleep, but decided he was only pretending so that they wouldn't have to talk.

Michael was haunted by the knowledge that if he had gone to the police the morning he first heard about Charlie Ward's death, Joe would not be in this mess. He wouldn't even be an accessory. Joe had done what he had because he believed he was protecting Michael. And Michael had never once tried to stop him.

It was already past six. But Michael knew better than to take Joe home when he'd been drinking. Instead he headed toward the highway, planning to find someplace to eat.

If he had been paying attention as he came up the entrance ramp, Michael might have noticed the white Toyota Tercel that was stopped in front of him at the Yield sign. But his mind was on Joe. So when the Tercel began to move forward, as if to merge, Michael, cruising up the ramp, barely hit the brake pedal, and looked in his side-view mirror for oncoming traffic. He did not see that the Tercel had suddenly, and unexpectedly, stopped again. When he did notice, it was too late. He slammed the brakes as hard as he could but slid into the Tercel's rear bumper anyway. The screech of brakes screamed through the hot summer air.

Joe bolted upright. "What the—"

"She was merging, then just stopped," Michael said, scarcely getting the words out without a stutter. "It's okay. I don't think there's any damage. I hardly hit it."

The person in the Tercel had not moved, probably startled by the impact and the sound of the Mustang's brakes. Michael backed up, pulled over to the edge of the ramp, and put on the four-way flashers. He wanted to see if the driver was okay. He was certain he hadn't hit her car hard. Still, he needed to make sure. But before he could open the door, Joe sprang from his side of the car and with enormous, purposeful strides headed toward the Tercel.

Michael looked on as Joe peered in the window of the driver's side, then jerked backward as if someone had suddenly pulled a gun on him. Before Michael realized what was happening, Joe jumped onto the hood of the Tercel and began to stomp on the windshield, alternating his feet, sometimes crashing down with both at once. He screamed at the girl in the car, calling her a crazy, stupid bitch, shouting until he was hoarse that she had almost wrecked his Mustang. Michael looked on in horror as fine weblike cracks spread through the glass.

Frantic, he ran toward the other car. "What the hell are you doing?" he shouted. But Joe did not seem to hear him. Again and again he brought his foot down on the windshield, until it began to cave in. Too terrified to think, Michael instinctively yanked open the car door to get the driver out before the glass caved in completely. And when he opened the door, he thought his heart might stop altogether. There, with her hands over her ears, eyes squeezed shut, screaming as loudly as she could, was Amy Ruggerio. With one final blow, the glass shattered around her, spraying tiny crystal shards that shimmered like sleet caught in her dark hair.

Michael put his hand around her arm and tried to pull her out, but she would not budge. She would not stop screaming. Maybe it was better if she didn't move, he decided. Glass was everywhere: in her lap, on her shoulders, on her thighs. It covered the dashboard, the seats, the floor. It lay like chipped ice on her feet, left vulnerable by thin-soled sandals.

Above him, Joe stood on the hood of the Tercel, his body slightly hunched forward, swaying in a kind of stupor. He looked lost and confused, as if he had no idea how he had come to be there. When Joe looked up, Michael saw with shock that his face was soaked with tears.

By now several cars had stopped, parking along the edge of the ramp, clicking on their own hazard lights. People Michael did not know were talking Joe down from the hood of the car, were carefully helping Amy from the driver's seat, gently picking glass from her hair, like apes grooming one another.

How could he have not recognized Amy's grandfather's car? Michael stumbled backward and sat down on the guardrail, feeling useless. He had done this. All of this. He had set it in motion. He suspected he was Joe's real target, that his friend's uncontrollable drunken rage was really meant for him. Amy had merely been in the wrong place at the wrong time. Like Charlie Ward.

He looked on as a woman in baggy orange shorts dusted glass from Amy's hair. Then, for a split second, Michael thought he saw Jenna Ward's face in Amy's stunned expression. Not in her features, but in her eyes. Something in Amy's eyes made him think of that first newspaper photograph of Jenna.

Michael swallowed hard. Everything was falling apart, shattering as surely as the windshield of the Tercel. And all he could do in that moment was sit helplessly by, surveying the wreckage, while strangers frantically tried to clean up the mess.

jenna

19

Jenna was standing only a few yards from the Ghost Tree when she saw her father. He was sitting next to Michael Mac-Kenzie, his head bowed in conversation only inches from the boy's. When her father saw her, he smiled and waved, beckoning her forward. Amy took her hand and pulled gently, but Jenna couldn't seem to move. She wasn't sure her legs would carry her. They felt as wobbly as two rubber bands. She began to scream at Amy to let her go.

Somewhere in the distance, she heard her mother's voice, felt a hand gently shaking her shoulder.

Jenna felt as if she were caught between two worlds. She struggled to answer the voice, but it was as if she were underwater and trying to talk to someone on the surface.

Someone was rocking Jenna back and forth. In the dream it was Amy who, more persistent than ever, was pushing her forward. But it was her mother's voice that Jenna kept hearing. She tried to open her eyes. Her lids ached with the effort.

"Jen?"

Jenna forced her eyes open and blinked.

Her mother was sitting on the edge of her bed. "I heard you cry out. I thought something was wrong."

"I did?" Jenna's tongue felt thick.

"Were you having a bad dream?"

Jenna closed her eyes and once again saw her father waving to her from beneath the Ghost Tree. "Yes. A bad dream."

"You want to talk about it?"

She shook her head. "I'm okay." Still disoriented, she began to massage her eyes. "What are you doing up?"

Her mother shrugged. "I was watching an old movie." She stared into the dimly lit hallway. "I don't seem to be sleeping very well these days."

Jenna didn't know what to say. So she simply put her hand on her mother's.

Meredith patted Jenna's hand and stood up. "I'd better try to get some rest. I've got two major meetings tomorrow morning." She stopped in the doorway. "If you need to talk, though, just wake me, okay?"

Jenna nodded. "Thanks."

Images of the dream continued to haunt her. So when she still hadn't fallen asleep an hour later, she crept downstairs to make a cup of herbal tea. She turned on the light above the stove and put the water on to boil, all the while thinking about this latest dream.

She rummaged through the numerous boxes of herbal tea, but nothing appealed to her. Instead she decided to make a cup of hot chocolate, although she could not have said why. Hot chocolate was for frosty nights. It was only early September.

Minutes later, sitting at the oak table, watching the steam rise from her cup, inhaling the rich smell of chocolate, she had a sudden vision of a younger Jenna holding out a gloved hand to take a Thermos mug of steaming hot chocolate from her father. She closed her eyes, and suddenly she was eleven years old again. She could see the Ghost Tree up ahead just as it had looked on that day four years before, the bare, mottled white branches shooting skyward in the frosty evening, made even whiter by the snow.

Her father had brushed the snow from the spot where three trunks grew out of a base that was as big around as a large kitchen table, making a seat for her. She had climbed into the tree and sat while he made a tent of bare branches and loose bark beneath a tight huddle of pine trees. The snow wasn't at all deep there. And when he was finished building the small shelter, he placed alfalfa and apples inside.

They had come to the Great Swamp to feed the animals, as they had every winter since she could remember. But this particular winter had been unusually harsh, and the deer were having a hard time finding food. Her father had wanted to create someplace sheltered to leave the apples and alfalfa so that if it snowed again, they wouldn't get buried. It was almost sundown, and he was hurrying because he didn't want them to be in the woods when it got dark.

The cold had chapped her cheeks, and her fingers stung inside her wool gloves, even though she held the steaming cup of hot chocolate her father had given her. But there in the cradle of the tree, watching the fiery glow of the setting sun as it dipped below the horizon, Jenna had felt warm and happy.

And later, as she and her father headed back to the car, he had told her the legend of the Ghost Tree. He said that no one really knew where it had come from. Some people claimed the Native Americans from the area, the Lenape tribe, had started the legend over three hundred years ago. The tree was that old. Even older, maybe.

The Lenape supposedly believed it was a sacred place where you could communicate with the spirits of your ancestors. But no one had the slightest idea whether the legend was true or not, because it was the white settlers who had given the old sycamore the name Ghost Tree. Legends sometimes got mixed up that way.

But her father had told her that according to the legend, if you spent the night in the cradle of the old sycamore, the spirits of your ancestors, all of them, from the beginning of time, would form circles around the tree, chanting their stories and sharing their wisdom with you as they danced through the night. It was, her father said, a place of healing.

Jenna stared down at her hot chocolate. She had taken only one swallow, and now it was lukewarm. She thought of going back to bed, but she knew she wouldn't be able to sleep. It was pointless to try to shut out the image of the Ghost Tree and the memories it had awakened. She wanted to understand why she was so haunted by this place. Because, in a strange way, she felt as if her life depended on it.

The next morning Jenna was surprised to find her mother still at home. It was Friday, a few days before Labor Day, and her mother had said she had important meetings that morning. Jenna stood in the doorway of her mother's bedroom, watching her fold a sweatsuit and put it in a large trash bag.

The windows were open, and the curtains swelled like gently billowing sails in the breeze. She welcomed the sounds of the traffic below as they mingled with the chirping of birds, grateful that the house no longer had the mausoleum chill of central air-conditioning.

"How come you're still home?" she asked.

When Meredith Ward looked over at her, Jenna saw that her eyes were puffy and wet. "I'm having a bad day."

"What about your meetings?"

"I asked someone to fill in for me."

Jenna sat down at the foot of the bed.

Her mother sat down next to her, clutching a sweater she had started to fold, and put her arm around her daughter. "It's so hard," she said. "So much harder than I ever imagined."

Jenna rested her head on her mother's shoulder. "Maybe you could talk to somebody, a—" She had been about to say a minister, but suddenly felt like a hypocrite. Her own feelings about God were still all mixed up with her anger and resentment. Even now, weeks after the accident, when people tried to comfort her with idiotic statements, telling her that her father's death was simply part of God's plan, she wanted to grab them by the shoulders and shake them until their eyes popped out.

She looked up at her mother's face and for the first time realized how terribly lonely her mother must be. It wasn't that she didn't have friends; she did. She went shopping at the mall with them, or to shows, or out to dinner. In fact, it seemed at times that there was some kind of conspiracy between them to keep their widowed friend busy. But Jenna knew that her mother's friends could never fill the void left by her father.

Her mother wiped her eyes with the sleeve of the sweater. "My friends have been good listeners," she said. A strand of damp hair clung to her cheek. She pushed it behind her ear and smiled. "And I have you."

Jenna lifted the balled-up sweater from her mother's hands. It was a burgundy wool crewneck Jenna had given her father two Christmases ago. She could still see him putting the sweater on right over his bathrobe, as if he couldn't wait to try it on. He had always made a big deal of her gifts.

Jenna was suddenly aware of the piles of clothing stacked all over the room: on the bed, the dresser, and even the floor. A trash bag sat on the floor by her mother's feet. "You're not throwing Daddy's things away, are you?" Jenna asked, alarmed.

"I'm not *throwing* his things away," her mother said. "I'm *giving* them away. To people who can use them. It's better than having them collect dust in the closet, isn't it?"

Jenna stroked her father's sweater as if it were a kitten curled up on her lap. She supposed giving her father's clothes to charity was the right thing to do.

She set the sweater back on the bed and wandered over to the walk-in closet. Her father's suits and shirts still lined one entire wall. Two months had passed since the accident. Yet it had never occurred to her that there would come a time when they would be giving away his clothes. "What about all Daddy's tools?" she asked. The workshop, his sacred space—were they going to pack that up, too?

Even with her back to her mother, Jenna heard her heavy sigh. "Maybe Mr. Krebs next door will want some of them, or maybe his son," she said. "Or I suppose we could have a yard sale or something."

Of course they wouldn't keep the tools. What would they do with them? Still, the thought of some stranger using them made Jenna want to cry. Brushing back tears, she lifted two of the suits from the metal bar, carried them over to the bed, and began to fold them.

"I think we should save the tools for a while." She glanced over at her mother. "Who knows, maybe I'll turn out to be pretty handy at fixing things. Maybe it's hereditary or something."

Meredith gently ran her thumbs over Jenna's damp cheeks. "I guess we could keep them for a while longer," she agreed.

Jenna suddenly remembered that she was supposed to

meet Andrea. They were going to the pool later that morning. But somehow being here, packing up her father's things, seemed more important. With each shirt she folded, with each sweater, with every pair of jeans, she found herself saying good-bye. Over and over, the silent goodbyes echoed in her heart, a goodbye to each and every thing, because she had never gotten the chance to say it on that fateful morning in July.

20

1ater that day, as Jenna and her mother were in the driveway loading up the Explorer with bags of Charlie Ward's clothes, Annie Rico hit them with the news. She pulled right up to the curb in her Isuzu Trooper and announced she was on her way home from the pharmacy and just had to see how Jenna and her mother were doing, "especially in light of the new developments."

Jenna and her mother exchanged bewildered looks and an unspoken question: What new developments? But neither of them said a word. They did not want Annie Rico to think they weren't up on things. So they waited.

"And to think he's only seventeen," Annie said. She began to fidget with a car deodorizer, shaped like an evergreen tree, that dangled from her rearview mirror.

Still they waited, although Jenna was beginning to think she might have to pull Annie right out of her car and shake her by the shoulders if she didn't get to the point soon. It was obvious that Annie knew something important about the investigation.

Meredith Ward smiled coolly. "Yes, it's a shame he's so young."

Jenna had to admire her mother's finesse. She actually sounded as if she understood what Annie Rico was babbling on about.

"Of course, they haven't formally pressed charges." Annie adjusted her rearview mirror and studied her bleached hair for a minute, tucking in a few loose strands that had somehow avoided an earlier assault from a can of hair spray. "But for heaven's sake, the police came right to his house and took him down to the station. They haven't done that with anyone else. So I'd have to say it doesn't look good for him."

"No, it doesn't," Meredith agreed.

"Well, keep me posted," Annie said, giving them a cheerful wave and steering her car away from the curb. As if Annie wouldn't know what was happening before anyone else, Jenna thought.

Jenna grabbed her mother's arm and shook it. "Mom! They caught him!"

"We don't know that for sure." Her mother stared down at the bulging plastic bag by her feet. Then, without warning, she bolted for the house.

Jenna was practically on her heels. But her mother returned to the front porch, cordless phone in hand, before Jenna even made it through the door. She sat down on the top step next to her mother and listened impatiently as she talked to Chief Zelenski. The conversation on her mother's end gave Jenna few clues. But she could tell that her mother was furious because no one had contacted them.

"Annie Rico," she was shouting over the phone. "We had to find out from Annie Rico. Can you imagine how we felt?"

When her mother finally pressed the Off button ten minutes later, Jenna could tell she was still upset. She hadn't seen her mother this angry in ages.

"Well, they caught him, didn't they?" Jenna had to fight back an urge to grab her mother's arm again.

"They took someone in for questioning, that's all." Her mother's voice was flat. She leaned forward, elbows poised on her knees, her chin resting in her hand. "Dave Zelenski seemed annoyed that I even knew about it," she said. "Can you believe that? He wanted to know how I'd found out." She flung her arms out. "So I told him, and what does he say? He tells me they haven't really arrested anyone. He said they're questioning a lot of people. It's routine."

"So they *didn't* catch him, then?" Jenna was disappointed, but even more than that, she was confused.

"I think they have a suspect, but they're not going to say anything until they're sure."

"So that's it?"

Her mother sighed. "For now, anyway."

Jenna picked up the cordless phone. "I'm going to call Andrea," she announced, heading for the front door, although that wasn't her plan at all. She was about to call Annie Rico, and she knew that if her mother found out, she'd be grounded for life.

But she was prepared to take that chance, because she had to find out the boy's name. Annie Rico had said he was only seventeen. Jenna realized for the first time that this boy could be someone she knew. Up until now her father's murderer had been a faceless monster. What if he turned out to be a monster with a familiar face? But as disturbing as that thought was, not knowing was even worse.

She headed up to her room, phone book under her arm, and when Annie Rico answered, all Jenna said was, "Do you know his name?"

There was a moment of silence. Then Annie's gravelly voice floated back to her. "Who is this?"

"Sorry, Mrs. Rico. This is Jenna Ward."

"Oh." There was another pause. "Whose name?"

Jenna squeezed her eyes shut. She hated this. Hated having to go to Annie Rico for information that should have been hers first. "The boy the police took in for questioning," Jenna said. "The police never told us his name. I thought maybe you'd know."

"Well, it just so happens I do."

Jenna stood there, twisting her hair around her finger, waiting. Was Annie going to make her beg, for pete's sake?

"Let me think, now. I know his mother. She comes into the pharmacy a lot. Buys a lot of herbs and vitamins. Real big on that health stuff."

Jenna was tapping her foot. What was this woman's problem?

"Ellen Sadowski. That's his mother. I think her youngest boy's name is Joe. Yes, that's it. Joe Sadowski. You know him? He probably goes to your school."

"No." Jenna breathed a sigh of relief, glad that the name wasn't familiar.

As soon as she hung up she began to flip through the telephone book again. Mrs. Rico had told them that this boy was the only person the police had actually taken to the station. That had to mean something. Jenna ran her finger along one of the pages. There was only one Sadowski family listed. They lived on Maple Avenue. Right in the four-block area that the police had been investigating.

"How soon till dinner?" Jenna asked, sticking her head into the kitchen, where her mother was washing chicken parts.

Her mother glanced up at the clock. "An hour, maybe. Depends on how long it takes to grill these." She held up a dripping wet chicken breast. "Why?"

"I'm going over to Andrea's. Okay?"

Without waiting for an answer, she headed out the sliding glass door and cut across the backyard to Andrea's house, although she had no intention of stopping there. Once she was on Andrea's street, Jenna began to run. Joe Sadowski lived on the other side of town. That was over a mile. And she had only an hour before she had to be home.

Thirty-three Maple Avenue. Jenna looked across the street at the modest ranch house. Much of the blue paint had been scraped away, and one side had already been repainted a pale yellow.

She leaned against one of the large maple trees that lined the street, watching the front door. She was hoping to get a glimpse of Joe Sadowski, although she had no idea what he looked like or what she would do if he suddenly came through the door.

Just then a boy rounded the corner, walking fast. At first she wondered if it was Joe; then she realized with a shock that it was Michael MacKenzie. He took off running across the Sadowskis' lawn. But for one brief moment he slowed his pace and looked across the street. She wondered if he had seen her. If he had, he gave no indication. He simply bounded up the front steps and rang the doorbell.

Jenna stepped behind the large maple. Her heart was thumping wildly. What was Michael MacKenzie doing at Joe Sadowski's house? She knew they were both seventeen and going to be seniors. But were they also friends?

She peeked around the tree to see what was happening. She felt ridiculous, as if she were playing some childish spy game. But she didn't care. She had to know what was going on. She watched as another boy, who she decided was Joe Sadowski, came to the door. At first she couldn't see him very well. But then he smacked the door open and stomped down the front steps, with Michael right behind him, and headed for the back of the house.

It was happening. She was staring right into the face of her father's murderer. Jenna could see that he was furious about something. He looked, she thought with a shudder, as if he could kill someone. And in that moment she realized she had seen his face before. She recognized the rolled-up bandanna he wore tied around his head. This was the boy who had been harassing Amy Ruggerio at Judd Passarello's party.

Jenna pulled back behind the tree to avoid being seen, then hid there until the two boys were out of sight. Michael, Amy, Joe . . . did they all know each other? She rested her forehead against the tree and closed her eyes. So what if they did? Did that really surprise her? After all, Briarwood was a small town; lives invariably collided, jostling other lives.

She was thoroughly disgusted with herself. She wasn't doing a thing, just standing there, staring, her thick lashes spiked with tears. She thought of her violent outburst at the beach, of Andrea's shock, of her conviction that she could confront her father's murderer and then, without remorse, point a gun in his face and fire. That had been a fantasy. This person, this boy across the street from her, was real. She knew now that no matter how much pain he had caused her, no matter how much she hated him, she would never be able to pull that trigger.

Jenna peeled the skin from a chicken leg and picked at the meat. The last thing she felt like doing was eating. Haunted by the images of Joe Sadowski and Michael MacKenzie, all she wanted was to get to the bottom of things. She wondered what Michael MacKenzie had been doing at Joe's. What, if anything, was his part in all this?

Her mother sat across the kitchen table from her, grinding coarse pepper onto her salad. She seemed equally preoccupied. She had barely said a word since Jenna had returned. Jenna suspected she had the investigation on her mind, too.

Jenna thought of calling Andrea to tell her what she'd found out, but realized that linking Michael MacKenzie with her father's murderer—if that was who Joe Sadowski was—would just upset her friend. There was no point in telling Andrea, not until Jenna had something concrete, anyway.

"What's going to happen to the boy who shot Dad?" she said.

"I don't know." Her mother was staring off into space, her eyes focused on some imaginary place over Jenna's head. "I don't want to see his life ruined. I mean, I realize what happened was an accident. And there's been enough pain already, don't you think? He's going to have to live with this for the rest of his life. I just want to know what happened. That's all. For my own peace of mind."

"Will he go to prison?"

"We don't even know if the boy they took in for questioning is the same person who fired the shot," her mother reminded her.

"But if he is?"

"Then I guess that will depend on whether it ever comes

to trial. They'll probably present it to a grand jury," her mother said. "When they have enough evidence."

"If they ever find any evidence."

"Well, if they do, and if he's found guilty, his sentence will depend on the judge. It could be suspended. Or he might have to do community service." Her mother paused. "Or he could go to prison."

Jenna wiped the barbecue sauce from her sticky fingers onto her napkin. Wasn't that what she wanted? To have this boy behind bars? She stared down at her half-eaten dinner. No matter what, if he'd killed her father, he was going to have to pay for what he'd done. "I think I'll go work a few math problems," Jenna told her mother, getting up from the table.

"Math problems? In the summer?"

Jenna shrugged. "School starts in a few days." It wasn't much of a reason, but she didn't feel like explaining that she sometimes used math problems to calm her thoughts.

A cool September breeze played with the pages of her algebra book as she lay in the hammock by the pool. The days were growing shorter, and already the sun had disappeared behind the treetops. Balancing the book on her raised knees, one arm pressed across the page to keep it from turning, she began to work on the first problem. She was counting on math to distract her from thinking about Joe Sadowski. But that wasn't happening. In fact, the questions that ran through her mind were more insistent than ever. For whenever she pictured Joe, she also saw Amy. And she found the connection disturbing.

Jenna stared down at a complex algebra problem without actually seeing it. Then it came to her. There was one common link in all this confusion, one person who just might have some answers for her: Amy Ruggerio.

michael

21

The afternoon the police came for Joe, Michael, as usual, was on duty at the pool. He would be relieved when the Labor Day weekend was over and he no longer had to come here. Because the word was out. The bullet that had killed Charlie Ward had come from the MacKenzies' backyard on the day of Michael's party. The police were questioning everyone who had been there.

For three days now, people had been coming up to Michael while he was supposed to be watching the swimmers, wanting to know if he knew who had fired that fatal shot. But no one dared to come right out and ask him if he had done it. He felt as if everyone were watching him, waiting for him to make a false move. His lifeguard stand was beginning to feel more and more like the witness stand in a courtroom trial.

Even worse, he found he could no longer sit on his stand, watching those in his charge, without his eyes coming to rest on the people whose lives he had in some way managed to screw up. Darcy came to the pool sometimes but usually stayed huddled in the middle of her group, refusing to look at him.

Amy showed up once in a while, on unbearably hot days

when the air was so heavy that it was difficult to breathe. But she hadn't been there since the car accident two days earlier.

If he closed his eyes, he could still see the police shoving Joe into the back of their cruiser. The scene was as vivid as if it were happening all over again that very minute. The emergency squad had arrived right after that, and the medics had ushered Amy, who kept insisting she was fine, into the back of the ambulance.

Michael had waited, giving the police all the information they required, accepting the ticket for careless driving as his due. Then he took Joe's car and followed Amy to the emergency room. But since no one would allow him in to see her, there was nothing to do but sit in the waiting room until she was discharged.

After what had seemed like the longest hour of his life, Michael saw Pappy coming toward him. He had managed to get a ride with a neighbor and had just come from seeing Amy.

"She's fine," he announced when he saw Michael. "A few minor cuts is all. I'm going to take her home."

Michael was relieved to hear that she was okay. "Can I see her?"

Pappy scratched at his goatee. "Probably not a good idea right now."

He had tried to call later that night, but Pappy had answered the phone. He explained that Amy had gone to bed early and he didn't want to wake her.

Michael scanned the pool without really seeing anyone. He couldn't concentrate. What if this latest fiasco had dealt the final blow to his relationship with Amy? Just when he'd thought she might give him another chance.

He shifted uncomfortably in his seat, then reached for the

sunblock to put on his nose. When he glanced up again, he spotted Jenna Ward sitting on the edge of the pool, talking with her dark-haired friend, the one she had wanted to introduce him to on the night of Judd Passarello's party. Michael still dreaded starting the new school year, still wondered how he was ever going to face Jenna in the halls. But he had grown accustomed to seeing her during the summer and had convinced himself that he could do it. He would do whatever it took just to keep going, because he didn't have a choice.

So when he came home that evening and Josh practically knocked him over at the back door with the news about Joe, Michael just stared him right in the eye and asked him if dinner was ready.

Josh took a step back, his mouth open. "Did you hear me? Joe's in jail," he repeated. "See, I was right! He's the killer."

Michael held his fist only a few inches from Josh's nose. "He's no killer, you little dork. So shut your stupid face." He unclenched his hand and let it drop to his side. "Got it?"

"Got it," Josh said, blinking wildly, just as Karen MacKenzie came through the back door with an armload of groceries.

She looked from Michael to Josh, then frowned. "Is something wrong?"

"They caught the killer," Josh said, not daring to look at his brother.

Karen MacKenzie sighed and brushed her damp hair away from her forehead. "They only took Joe in for questioning," she told him. "He wasn't arrested."

"But everybody's pretty sure he did it," Josh said, growing excited again.

His mother set the bag of groceries on the kitchen counter and began to empty it. "It's wrong to just assume someone's guilty," she told Josh. "The police are only trying to get to the bottom of this. They're questioning a lot of people." She shifted her glance to Michael.

He noticed how drawn and tired her face looked. There were dark smudges beneath her eyes. It occurred to him that maybe she hadn't been getting much sleep since Healey and Boyle had found that casing in the backyard. And why should she? No matter how any of this turned out, his mother knew the rifle had been fired from her backyard while she had been overseeing the party. For the first time Michael realized that his parents probably held themselves responsible for Charlie Ward's death.

His mother was watching him. Michael felt a tingling in the tips of his fingers. He wondered if she suspected something. But she only said, "Joe's going to be fine. I called his mother from work as soon as I heard. He should be home by now. Why don't you give him a call?"

Michael said he'd do that—although he had absolutely no intention of calling Joe—and then headed straight for his room. He needed someplace to think. He couldn't believe Healey and Boyle had talked to all forty of his friends already. He had thought it would take weeks. Or were they just questioning Joe the way they were everyone else? Maybe this was simply part of the investigation. But he knew better. Friends of his at the pool, who had been at his party, had told him the police had come to their homes, asked a few questions, and that was it. This was different. The police had taken Joe down to the station. He was definitely a major suspect.

Michael couldn't stop thinking about him. He wondered how Joe had handled things, or if he had told the cops anything. Maybe they had broken him down, gotten a confession out of him. For all he knew, they might come knocking on

Michael's own door any minute with a warrant for his arrest. He finally decided that he couldn't just sit there hiding in his room. He had to know what had happened.

He headed back downstairs. "I'm going over to Joe's," he called into the kitchen as he pushed open the front screen door. "I'll be back in time for dinner."

He knew he could have called Joe, but he was afraid the police might have tapped his phone. He was probably being paranoid, but he didn't want to take any chances.

A few minutes later, as he hurried across Joe's front lawn, something caught Michael's attention. He barely glanced across the street, preoccupied with what he was going to say to Joe. But in that single moment he thought he saw Jenna Ward standing by a tree. Badly shaken, he climbed the front steps of Joe's house and rang the bell. Then he sneaked a furtive look over his shoulder. No one was across the street. *Man, you really are paranoid,* he thought.

His mother had been right; Joe was home. When he came to the front door, he just stood there, staring at Michael. Finally he said, "You sure you want to be seen with a hardened criminal?"

Michael winced. "I thought they just took you in for questioning. They didn't actually arrest you, did they?"

"You're right. They didn't." Joe sneered. "Does that make you feel better?"

Michael peered around Joe, squinting into the dark foyer to see if anyone was listening. "Maybe we shouldn't talk here," he said.

"Do we have something to talk *about?*" Joe's face was absolutely expressionless.

Michael felt the weight of his friend's words on Michael's chest. He would have turned away, gone home right then, but his need to know what had happened at the police station was stronger than his sense of loss and humiliation. "I think we do," he said, trying to sound in control.

Joe banged open the screen door with his fist and headed around to the backyard. Michael was right on his heels. He suspected Joe was going to the tree house. These days the old tree house was really no more than a wood platform with two walls and half a roof. The ladder that led to it was missing several rungs. Michael wondered why the Sadowskis had never torn it down. All their kids were grown up and had left home, except for Joe, who was the youngest. And besides, the tree house was a real eyesore. Still, it was a place where he and Joe could go to talk, just as they had when they were small boys, and no one would overhear their conversation.

Joe climbed the ladder, sat down cross-legged, and lit a cigarette.

Michael sat across from him. "I thought you gave those things up."

"What's it to you?" Joe said, exhaling a stream of smoke in Michael's direction.

This was not going to be a long conversation. Michael knew he had to ask what he had come for and then leave. He could tell that Joe was barely able to stand the sight of him. "So what happened down there? They didn't try to pin anything on you, did they?"

Joe pulled his knees up close to his chest and took another drag from his cigarette, squinting to keep the smoke from burning his eyes. "I stuck to our original story, if that's what you're worried about." He shook his head. "Man, how many times do I have to tell you? Without the gun, they ain't got a case. They couldn't arrest me because they don't even have circumstantial evidence. Just a stupid hunch." Joe flicked his ashes over the edge.

"So why did they bring you in for questioning?" Michael still couldn't understand it. Especially if the cops really didn't have anything to go on. "Why didn't they just talk to you here, like last time?"

"Who knows?" There was a definite edge to Joe's voice. "They wanted to know why I took so long filing that report for the stolen gun. Then they started harping on how there wasn't any damage to my car. They said it was a pretty clean robbery. No signs of a break-in."

Michael noticed the thin mustache of sweat on Joe's upper lip. When he lifted the cigarette to his lips, his hand trembled. Whatever had gone on down at the police station had really shaken him up. "So what did you tell them?" Michael asked.

Joe ran his thumbnail along his upper lip. "I said for all I knew, I'd left the damn car unlocked. I said I couldn't remember that far back."

"That's still not enough reason to take you down to the station," Michael said.

Joe was squinting through the smoke. "Seems I got quite a reputation with the local powers that be. First they pick me up from the scene of a car accident, drunk. Then they charge me with being drunk and disorderly and with assault for stomping in that stupid bitch's windshield." He flicked more ashes over the side. "Let's face it, man, I ain't exactly their candidate for mayor."

At the mention of Amy, Michael felt a rush of anger. But then Joe started talking again, and Michael backed off.

"Besides, a couple of kids from the party told them I was

messing around with your rifle that day." Joe stared Michael right in the eye.

"Why would anyone say that?" Michael was certain the only time Joe had even held the gun was when they were in the woods.

"Because it's true, man." He rubbed one eye with his palm. "You were off making it with that pig. Jeez, I just wanted to look at it."

This time when Joe brought up Amy, Michael grabbed him by the front of his T-shirt. He almost threw him over the side. "Lay off Amy," he warned.

Joe gave him an ugly sneer. "I think *lay* is the operative word here."

Michael would have slammed his fist right into Joe's face if it hadn't suddenly sunk in that Joe had just confessed to being seen at the party with the rifle. Now a muddle of questions flooded his mind. Had Joe fired the gun that day without Michael's knowledge? If he had, then maybe he, Michael, wasn't the one who had killed Charlie Ward. He let go of Joe's shirt.

"You said you had my Winchester that day?" he asked, trying not to sound as if he was accusing Joe of anything.

"I was looking at it," Joe said. "I picked it up, that's all. I didn't do anything with it." He squashed the cigarette on the weathered boards.

Michael was still staring down at the smoking butt when he heard Mr. Sadowski's voice below telling Joe that the police were there with a search warrant and that he'd better get himself inside. *Fast.* Suddenly Michael was eleven years old again and Mrs. Sadowski was peering over the top of the tree house ladder, her face contorted in fury, screaming at him and Joe for sneaking a can of beer from the refrigerator. They had been sitting there, the half-empty can between them like a warm campfire, until they'd been caught.

"They think you've got the gun hidden here," Michael said when he could collect his thoughts.

"No kidding, Sherlock." Joe stood up and stared down at him with disgust. "They think I'm their man," he said. "But they ain't going to find a thing. My dad's attorney was at the station with me this afternoon. He says they need hard evidence. And as far as I'm concerned, they ain't got diddly-squat."

It had gone this far. Mr. Sadowski's attorney had been there. Michael realized he would probably be needing an attorney himself soon. "What did you tell him? Your attorney, I mean."

Joe snorted, then shook his head. "I told him I didn't fire the gun at the party. I said I didn't even have the stupid gun. I told him the truth, man." Joe stared up at the sky through the missing section of roof. He seemed to be thinking about something. "I asked him, though, just for jollies, what would happen to the person who did it."

Michael did not want to hear what was coming next. It was all he could do to keep from leaping over the side of the tree house and taking off at a run. But Joe was staring him down again, and he didn't dare move a muscle.

"He said he'd probably be charged with involuntary manslaughter, which is pretty much what we figured in the first place—unless, of course, he was stupid enough to try to conceal the evidence, which, it seems, would be an obstruction of justice. The judge might not be so understanding in that case."

Michael massaged his forehead. His head had begun to ache. "What about that report you filed?"

"Filing a false police report ain't exactly gonna make their day, either." Joe lowered himself onto the first rung of the ladder. "Oh, yeah, there's this other thing. Shooting that gun off like you did. They'll nail you for that, too. Illegal discharge of a firearm."

Michael hadn't said a word. His mouth was as dry as sand. He wanted to tell Joe that they'd been wrong, that they should have gone to the police that morning as soon as they heard the announcement on the radio. But there didn't seem to be much point in bringing that up now. So he said nothing.

Joe was watching him, a twisted grin on his face.

"If they arrest you," Michael said, licking his lips, "I mean, if they think they've got a case or something, I'm going to tell them the truth."

Joe snickered. "Sure you will," he said, backing down the ladder. "Any way you look at it, we're dead."

ichael had fully intended to go right home. He knew his mother would have dinner ready by now. But he didn't feel much like eating. All he could think about was Joe.

It troubled him that Joe hadn't told him about the gun sooner, about picking it up when Michael wasn't around. He wondered what else Joe might be hiding. There was no telling what was going on in his mind anymore, no way to predict his behavior. He was a walking time bomb.

Michael had begun to entertain the possibility that he wasn't a murderer after all. Maybe it had been Joe all along. Maybe Joe had shot the Winchester while Michael and Amy were in the garage.

He thought back to that morning in July when they had first learned of Charlie Ward's death. He remembered how Joe had insisted that Michael hide the evidence, and how persistent he had been about not going to the police.

Then he'd started talking about doing things he wasn't proud of. Michael wondered now what Joe had meant by that. Was it possible that he'd been talking about firing the gun that killed Charlie Ward and letting Michael believe it was his fault?

Yet even as he tried to shift the blame to Joe, he knew in his heart that his friend hadn't done it.

Even if Joe *had* fired the gun while Michael was in the garage with Amy, the bullet wouldn't have been the one that killed Charlie Ward. Michael and Amy had been together later in the afternoon, at least an hour after the accident had taken place.

But it still looked bad for Joe. He couldn't keep the cops at bay with the same old story for much longer. Maybe they didn't have any hard proof yet, but it seemed pretty obvious they were working overtime to build a case out of circumstantial evidence.

Michael struggled to think straight. He needed to come up with a plan. He couldn't let Joe take the rap for Charlie Ward's death. Or could he? He knew that even though Joe hadn't done it, and even if it never came to trial for lack of evidence, most folks would think Joe was guilty anyway. People were like that sometimes. They had to have someone to blame. It would be the easiest thing in the world to let them believe what they wanted. It was the perfect setup, really. And he knew it.

for a while Michael wandered aimlessly up one street and down another with no particular destination in mind. That is, until he came to Amy's street. And as he rounded the corner and saw the small white house at the end of the road, he realized this was the one place where he had known the only moments of peace he had found that summer. Maybe he was kidding himself. Maybe it *was* hopeless. But he had to keep trying.

The white Tercel sat in the driveway. Its new windshield caught the last rays of the setting sun. Michael stood looking at the car, remembering the day of the accident. And because he no longer expected anything, because he had lost all hope, he was not prepared for the touch of a hand on his shoulder or, as he spun around, to find Amy standing behind him. He was so stunned, he could barely breathe.

Amy did not smile. And Michael thought he recognized something of his own pain and loneliness reflected in her face.

He tipped his chin in the direction of the car. "They got that fixed pretty fast." It was all he could think of to say.

Amy looked over at the Tercel. "Pappy's got friends in the business."

Michael shoved his hands in his pockets and leaned against the car. "Why did Joe do it? Smash your windshield, I mean."

"I don't know. Because he'd been drinking, I guess." Amy combed her fingers through her hair and stared down at her feet. Then she looked back at the house as if she were expecting someone to come through the door.

"You know . . ." Amy paused and squeezed her eyes closed. She seemed unsure whether or not to continue. Then she looked him straight in the eye and said, "Joe told me once why he'd brought me to your party. He said you wanted to get it on with me. He said I was his birthday present to you." Her eyes began to tear.

"Why would he say something like that?" Michael's heart began to race.

"I don't know. Maybe because he was drunk when he told me. Or maybe because it's true."

He could hardly believe what he was hearing. "I told you

217

before, I didn't even know he was bringing you to my party."

Amy watched him for a few seconds without saying anything. "But we ended up in your garage anyway."

"Amy . . ."

"So it was just about sex, right?"

He understood now that this was what Amy had been trying to find out that evening in the 7-Eleven parking lot a few days earlier. "Look, Amy . . . I don't know what you want me to say. I mean, you looked so good in that bathing suit. . . . Maybe it *was* about sex at first. I didn't know you then. But it isn't like that now. You know? I really care about you." He spread his hands. "I'm sorry you had to go through this. With Darcy and all. It stinks, and I feel rotten about it. I don't know what else to say."

Amy folded her arms and looked over at the windshield.

Michael was still trying to understand why Joe would even tell Amy such a thing in the first place. Was he trying to get back at Michael because he felt Michael was letting him take all the blame for the accident? Did Joe really hate him that much?

Michael felt so betrayed that he didn't care if Joe *was* accused of the murder. *Let* him take the blame! Nobody would take Joe's word over his. He didn't owe him anything anymore.

Yet even when he attempted to transfer the burden of his guilt to Joe, he felt no relief. How could he wish this pain, the same pain he had lived with for almost two months, on a friend? Even if that friend had grown to hate him. He would not wish that on anyone.

"The police were here this afternoon." Amy's soft voice floated up to him.

Michael knotted his hands into fists and stared up at the

sky. He did not dare look at Amy because he knew that her face would have the same open, trusting expression she always wore.

"They're questioning everyone who was at my party."

"That's what they said."

Michael jerked his thumb at the car. "I'm sorry," he said. "I didn't mean for any of this to happen."

Amy nodded. "I know," she whispered.

She looked so beautiful standing there, with the light from the sunset spilling across her face. Michael desperately wanted to touch her, but he didn't dare. He knew he should probably leave. He'd done what he came for. He had apologized face-to-face. But he wanted more than that. He wanted them to be like they had been before. And there wasn't a thing he could say or do to make that happen.

Amy turned to go. She was heading up the front walk. And he was doing nothing to stop her.

"There's something you should know about me," Michael called after her. He felt his throat swell and wondered if he would be able to get the rest of the words out. "Something . . . really rotten."

Amy stopped and looked over her shoulder. She seemed to be searching his face. Then she said, her voice scarcely above a whisper, "I'm not the person you should be telling."

Michael's blood went cold; his skin prickled with sweat. "What do you mean?" he said, terrified of what she was going to say.

"I was there, remember. At your party. The day that shot was fired."

Michael's body had tipped slightly forward, as if he were waiting for her to strike him. "Yeah?"

"I saw you come out of the woods with the rifle. Joe was with you." Tears had begun to form at the corners of her eyes.

"But I didn't really make the connection until I heard that the police were talking to the people who'd been at your party. Or maybe I did, but I didn't want to think about it."

"You saw me?" Michael was so shocked, he couldn't think straight. Amy had seen him with the rifle. And like everyone else in town, she had known that Charlie Ward had been shot by a stray bullet on the Fourth of July. Yet never once during all those weeks had she questioned him. Or judged him.

He wondered if she had told the police what she had seen. If she had, they would have come to *his* house instead of Joe's. They would have taken him into custody as a major suspect. But that hadn't happened. At least not yet.

If Amy had withheld crucial information, that would make her an accessory, too, like Joe. Michael cringed at the thought. But he couldn't bring himself to ask her outright what she had told the police.

Michael leaned back against the Tercel for support and covered his eyes with his hand. He could face Joe's anger and resentment. And he would face the police when the time came. But Amy, who trusted and believed in him—that was something else. He wanted to die.

He did not expect to feel Amy's arms around him. Not ever again. But when she slipped her hands under his arms and began to stroke the back of his neck, all he could do was press his face into her hair and cry.

jenna

for almost an hour Jenna had been watching Amy and trying to get up the courage to speak to her. Even now, in broad daylight, surrounded by all her friends at the pool, she was having difficulty separating the Amy who appeared in her dreams with the person who, less than a hundred feet away, was rummaging through a purple paisley tote bag.

Andrea, toweling her wet hair, sat next to Jenna. Jenna had not told her anything about what she had found out the night before. And now, watching her friend dry her hair without even once taking her eyes off Michael MacKenzie, Jenna knew she had done the right thing.

Almost all of their friends were at the pool that morning, although Jason was noticeably absent. It was Labor Day weekend, and the pool would be closed after Monday.

Jenna knew full well how Andrea and the others would react if she suddenly got up and walked over to where Amy sat. She thought of calling Amy at home and talking to her on the phone, but somehow that seemed too impersonal, given what she wanted to ask her. She thought of meeting Amy somewhere. The mall, perhaps. But then she'd have to wait even longer to talk to her, and she'd already waited a whole sleepless night.

Why did everyone have to treat Amy like a pariah, anyway? It was so stupid. She didn't seem at all like the person who was the butt of so many vicious rumors and jokes. She'd never been anything but kind, as far as Jenna could tell.

Fine. Let them think what they want, Jenna decided, getting to her feet. And without saying a word to Andrea or the others, she simply marched right over to Amy and sat down on the edge of her beach towel.

Amy was reading a magazine, but she closed it, letting it rest on her thighs when Jenna sat down.

Jenna already knew what she was going to say—something she should have said weeks ago. "I wanted to thank you for your letter."

Amy tossed the magazine on the grass next to her. Two dark smudges remained on her thighs where the ink from the back page had stuck to the suntan oil. "I thought it might help."

"It did." Jenna felt awkward. She wasn't at all sure what to say next. Finally she took a deep breath and said, "I'm sorry about what happened to your parents."

Amy rubbed at the inky spots on her legs. "It was a long time ago."

"I guess it never really stops hurting, though."

Amy's smile was sympathetic. "Maybe it does for some people." She brushed her hair away from her face. "I think the hardest part for me was the guilt."

"Guilt?" Jenna felt a strange tingling throughout her body. She recognized the prickly sensation that preceded the panicky feelings she usually had around Jason.

"Yes, guilt," Amy said. "For a long time I felt guilty about being the one who survived."

When Jenna looked confused, Amy added, "I was in the car when they had the accident."

Jenna shook her head but never once took her eyes from Amy's. She wanted to say something, to give something back for the letter Amy had written her. But there didn't seem to be anything she could say. Nothing that wouldn't sound empty and stupid.

The conversation was growing more and more difficult, leading to places Jenna did not want to go. She tried to focus her attention on something else. Out of the corner of her eye, Jenna saw Andrea staring at her, her lips parted in surprise. Her eyes were wide with disapproval. Jenna shifted her body so that she wouldn't have to see what was going on behind her back.

She needed to change the subject. She wanted to ask about Joe Sadowski, but she wasn't at all sure how to go about it. Amy seemed to be waiting.

"I was wondering . . . ," Jenna began cautiously. "That night at Judd Passarello's party, this guy seemed to be harassing you. I saw you in the dining room with him." She hesitated. "Was that Joe Sadowski?"

Amy didn't answer right away. She seemed to be concentrating hard on something. "Do you know him?"

Jenna said, "No, but I've heard a few things."

Amy licked her lips and folded her arms around her raised knees. "What kind of things?"

This was going all wrong. Amy was not answering her questions. Instead *she* was asking questions, questions Jenna had no answers for. She switched tactics. "He's a friend of Michael MacKenzie's, right?" She tilted her head toward Michael's lifeguard stand when she said this, only to meet his gaze head-on. He was not wearing his sunglasses, and she could see that he was looking right at them. And not just a casual glance.

He was staring openly. Did he sense they were talking about him?

Amy had been looking in the same direction. Now she took a deep breath. "You know Michael?"

"Not personally." Jenna suddenly remembered Amy standing in the front doorway at Judd Passarello's party, watching her. "I only talked to him once," she added.

Amy got to her feet. She tossed her magazine into the tote bag and began gathering up her other things. "I have to go," she said.

The sunlight glinting off the pool water had begun to hurt Jenna's eyes. Her sunglasses were back on her towel. She shaded her eyes with her hand, looking up at Amy. Amy was leaving, and she hadn't answered a single question. Jenna was so frustrated, she thought she might cry. She stood, picked up the beach towel, and handed it to Amy.

Amy didn't bother to fold it. She simply bunched it into a ball and stuffed it in her bag. Then she surprised Jenna by putting her hand on Jenna's shoulder. Jenna was suddenly reminded of her dream. "You think Joe had something to do with your father's death, don't you?"

Jenna's heart skipped a beat. "I don't know," she whispered.

"I guess by now everyone in town knows he's a potential suspect," Amy said. "It's no secret."

Jenna wasn't sure she could bring herself to ask the next question. Amy was watching her. And Jenna knew from the look on her face that she had already anticipated what Jenna would say.

Before Jenna even opened her mouth, Amy said simply, "No. I don't think he did it." Then she turned to leave, the tote bag bouncing gently against her hip. When she had gone only a few steps, she stopped and looked back at Jenna. "I'm sorry I wasn't more help."

Jenna watched her walk away. Amy had been her last chance at getting some answers. And those answers were there—she had sensed it. Amy had not been totally open with her. Jenna could see it in her eyes. She wished that she had thought to ask Amy if she had ever heard of the Ghost Tree and if she had ever dreamt about it. Now it was too late.

Disappointed, she started back to her towel. And when she glanced over at Michael MacKenzie, she was startled to discover that he was still watching her. Even from where she stood, she could see deep creases in his forehead. He was obviously disturbed about something.

Although her thoughts were preoccupied with Joe Sadowski and Michael MacKenzie, Jenna still worried about Jason. Even while she and Andrea roamed about the mall that afternoon, and all during Andrea's incessant chatter about Michael, Jason kept creeping into Jenna's thoughts.

So when he showed up at her front door that night, Jenna didn't know what to think. Jason never just "dropped by." He always called first. And he hadn't even been to her house since Judd Passarello's party.

What was he doing there now? Jenna had thought their relationship was over. But there he stood, in his frayed cutoffs and Led Zeppelin T-shirt, his hair as wild and unruly as ever, asking if she wanted to go for a walk.

"A walk?" Jenna said, stalling for time while she tried to think of some reason she couldn't leave the house.

"Yeah," Jason said, "a walk. You know, that's where you put one foot in front of the other and your body moves from one place to the next."

Jenna grinned at him. "Very funny."

Jason jammed his hands in his pockets and shrugged. "I try."

For one brief moment she had almost forgotten the now familiar feeling of dread she had whenever she was near him. Jason was smiling at her through the screen. It seemed, at least for one normal minute, like the old days. Before the accident.

"Come on," he said, resting his hand on the doorknob. "It's just a walk."

And because Jenna couldn't think of an excuse that didn't sound totally ridiculous, she shouted to her mother that she was going out with Jason for a while. Jason looked relieved when she stepped out onto the front porch, as if he hadn't been at all sure she would come with him.

It was a cool evening, and although it wasn't quite seven-thirty, the last of the sun's rays had already disappeared behind the trees as Jenna and Jason rounded the corner at the end of the block. She still felt anxious, but she was working hard to keep it under control.

"We didn't get to finish talking last week at Judd's party," Jason said finally.

Jenna's breath caught in her throat. "I thought you didn't want to talk anymore. You walked off, remember?"

They had wandered into the playground of the elementary school two blocks from Jenna's house. Jenna sat down on one of the swings. Jason took the swing next to her.

"Have I done something?" he asked.

"Like what?"

"I don't know. You tell me."

"You haven't done anything," Jenna said, trying to reassure him. "This has nothing to do with you." Although of course it did, because of the way she felt whenever she was around him. But how was she supposed to explain something she didn't understand herself? "It's just me," she said.

"Can you be a little more specific, Jen?" Jason was hunched forward, his elbows resting on his knees, his hands clasped together. He looked lost.

Jenna felt so awful that she finally gave in and told him about the anxiety attacks. If he wanted to think she was losing her mind, then fine. At least he wouldn't go on blaming himself.

Jason listened quietly. He did not interrupt her even once. And when she finished her story, all he could do was groan.

Jenna watched him, waiting to see what he would say.

"How am I supposed to fight something like this? I mean, another guy, yeah. That's one thing. But this?"

"There's nothing to fight."

"There is if I want things to work out for us."

Poor Jason. He wasn't going to give up. Jenna felt an overwhelming urge to take his hand. But that would only make matters worse.

"So why is this happening?"

Jenna grabbed hold of the chains and began to gently swing back and forth. "I haven't got a clue."

The look on Jason's face was painful to see as he sat watching her pump the air with her legs, lifting the swing higher and higher.

Jenna let her head fall back. The wind in her hair felt absolutely delicious. She had forgotten how good it felt to swing. She thrust her legs forward, flying out as far as she could.

Jason's voice drifted up to her. "You know, I always thought it was really weird that I didn't find out about what happened to your dad until weeks after the accident."

"What are you talking about?" Jenna said, calling down to him. "You weren't even there. How could you have known?"

"No. I mean, don't you think it's strange that we were talking on the phone one minute, and the next minute your dad gets shot, and I didn't even know about it? I was probably outside helping load the last of the camping equipment in the van or something. And there you were, outside . . ."

Jenna lurched forward and at the same time felt the seat of the swing slip out from under her. It happened so fast that she scarcely had time to react. One minute she was swinging her way up to the evening star; the next she was struggling to clutch one of the chains as her legs treaded air, then scraped along the pavement below. The seat wobbled back and forth, bumping her knees, but she clung to the chain for dear life.

Jason had his arms around her, lifting her away from the bruising wood seat. He held her tight, and he wasn't about to let go.

"What happened?" he whispered.

Jenna felt his breath on her ear. "I slipped."

Neither of them said anything for a while. Jenna had her face pressed against Jason's familiar shoulder. And not once did she think about the anxiety attacks.

Finally Jason asked, "Was it because of what I said?"

She leaned back and looked at him. "About what?"

"About the phone call."

Her legs began to feel unsteady. She needed to sit down, so she lowered herself to the ground, right there on the pavement. Jason sat down beside her. "I'd forgotten we were talking on the phone that day," she said.

"It was around lunchtime," Jason reminded her. "I remember because my mom shoved a bologna sandwich in my hand while you and I were talking. She was nagging me to get off the phone so we could get on the road."

"Lunch," Jenna whispered. Tears were beginning to sting the corners of her eyes. She was remembering, and she was not at all sure she could handle what was coming.

"What is it?" Jason said, taking her hand.

"My mom was nagging me, too. She wanted me to hang up and call Dad to lunch." She had begun to cry openly now, as once more she saw her mother standing at the kitchen counter making tuna fish sandwiches. And then she was looming over Jenna, telling her to get off the phone and get her dad. Her mother had asked her at least three times, but Jenna was used to that. Three times was nothing. She usually held out until her mother threatened to grab the phone out of her hand.

This was what she hadn't been able to remember the morning Chief Zelenski came to take their statements. "Oh, Jason," she moaned between tearful hiccups. "If I'd gotten off the phone when Mom asked, my dad would still be alive."

"Hey," he said. "Don't do this, okay?" He pulled her onto his lap and stroked her hair while her tears soaked the front of his T-shirt. "You can't blame yourself."

She kept her face buried against his chest. "But it *is* my fault," she insisted. "If I'd done what I was told, he would have been sitting at the kitchen table, eating his sandwich, when that bullet landed." Suddenly Amy's voice echoed in Jenna's ears: *"I think the hardest part for me was the guilt."*

"Okay, so then it's my fault, too," Jason was saying. "Because I wouldn't let you get off the phone. I didn't want you to go."

Jenna sat up and looked at him. "Oh, Jason," she whispered, wiping the tears from her cheeks, "it isn't your fault."

"Maybe that's why you didn't want to be with me anymore."

"But I'd forgotten all about that phone call," she reminded him.

"Consciously, maybe."

Jenna sighed and stared up at the sky.

"Hey, think about it," he said when she didn't respond. "I mean, people hide things from themselves all the time, you know? Stuff they can't deal with."

"So you think being around you reminded me of that day?"

"Why not? It's possible."

Jenna stood up and brushed loose gravel from her shorts and bare legs. She had a few scrapes on her knees, but they were not bleeding much. "I don't blame you for any of this," she told him. "I was the one who wouldn't get off the phone. It's my fault he's dead."

She knew she would have to find a way to tell her mother, even if it meant her mother ended up hating her, because Jenna couldn't live in the same house with her, harboring such a dark secret.

She and Jason began to walk back toward her street. And when Jason took her hand, Jenna waited for her skin to prickle with sweat and her heart to pound so hard it would stop her breath. But when this didn't happen, when all she felt was the soft night air on her cheeks and Jason's gentle touch, she inched a little closer to him and never once let go of his hand.

24

Her mother was already in bed, reading a book, a large bowl of popcorn by her side, when Jenna came into the bedroom later that night. She sat down at the foot of the bed.

Meredith held up the bowl. "Want some?"

Jenna helped herself to a handful of popcorn. She had come to tell her mother the truth. To tell her how she was responsible for her father's death. She wanted to tell her mother how sorry she was for everything that had happened. But she had no idea where or how to begin.

If there was anything good that had come out of all this tragedy, it was that for a while, anyway, Jenna and her mother had begun to grow closer. Over the past two months they had somehow managed to put aside their differences through an unspoken agreement. And Jenna found that she was grateful for this fragile truce. Now she couldn't help wondering if that was about to change. She had no idea how her mother was going to react. So she tried to brace herself for anything: shock, tears, outrage. She fully expected her mother to hate her.

Meredith pulled back the covers on the other side of the bed. She patted the space beside her. Jenna kicked off her shoes and wiggled down beneath the blankets. She felt five years old again. She took another handful of popcorn, glad to have something to keep her mouth occupied.

"Is something wrong?" her mother asked.

It was eerie the way her mother could sense things like that. Jenna looked at her and nodded. "I have to tell you something. When I was with Jason tonight . . ." She stopped. How could she tell anyone, especially her mother, what she'd found out?

"Are you and Jason having problems?"

Jenna shook her head. "No. Well, at first, but . . ." She tried to explain about the panic attacks, how she had felt whenever she was around Jason lately. But it wasn't coming out right.

Her mother inched closer to Jenna and put her arm around her. "You don't have to talk about it if you don't want to," she said gently. "I just wish you had let me know about these attacks earlier. Why don't I call Dr. Campbell tomorrow and make an appointment for you? Maybe he can help."

"Mom, you don't understand. I think the attacks are gone now. Because I know what caused them." Jenna began kneading the blanket with her fingers.

"What?" Meredith stroked Jenna's hair.

"It's my fault Daddy's dead," Jenna said, forcing back the tears because she did not want sympathy. She didn't deserve it. "And I'm sorry. Really, truly sorry."

Her mother looked confused. She shook her head. "What in the world are you talking about?"

So Jenna told her what had happened earlier that evening, what she had finally remembered about the day her father died. All those details that she hadn't been able to remember when Chief Zelenski questioned her. Then she waited, not knowing what to expect. But her mother only folded Jenna into her arms and continued to stroke her hair.

"We're a fine pair," she whispered. "Taking on all this blame."

Jenna pulled away and looked at her mother. "We?"

Meredith Ward took the bowl of popcorn and set it on the floor next to the bed. "For weeks I've been thinking that if I'd gone outside and called Charlie myself, instead of waiting for you to do it, I could have saved him. I keep thinking maybe none of this would have happened."

"But Mom, I'm the one who wouldn't get off the phone," Jenna said.

Her mother held up her hand, as if to stop her from saying anything more. "I know what you're like when you get on the phone with your friends. It's almost impossible to get you off. I should have thought of that. I should have gone outside and called him myself. And there was that list. What if I'd never asked him to fix the roof? What if I'd hired someone to do it? What if—"

"Oh, Mom." Jenna sighed. "You didn't have any way of knowing what would happen."

"And neither did you." Her mother gave Jenna's hand a squeeze and smiled. "Let's not do this, okay? Your dad loved you. I don't think he'd want either of us blaming ourselves like this."

"I can't help it. I can't help feeling he'd be alive if it weren't for me."

"If it weren't for someone carelessly shooting off a gun," Meredith reminded her. "You didn't pull that trigger, Jen. You need to keep things in perspective. Don't punish yourself for something you had no control over."

Jenna thought about the person who *had* pulled the trigger. The boy who had killed her father. Maybe her mother had been right the other day. That boy would have to live with what he'd done for the rest of his life. Just as Jenna knew she would have to live with what she *hadn't* done.

"It doesn't look good for him," Jenna told her mother. "Joe Sadowski, I mean."

Meredith sighed. "I know. I've heard rumors that the police were at the Sadowski house last night with a search warrant. Apparently everybody in town knows about it."

"Annie Rico?"

"Of course."

They both laughed.

"Mom?"

"Mmm?"

"Someone I know . . . a friend . . . told me he didn't do it."

Her mother frowned. "Does this person know something she should be telling the police?"

"I don't know. But the thing is, I think I believe her."

"Well, from what I've heard, most of what the police have is barely even circumstantial. So your friend may be right."

Jenna listened to her mother as she went on to speculate about the boy who might have fired the gun. But Jenna could not seem to let go of her own part in the tragedy, even though her mother had tried to assure her that none of what had happened was her fault.

And there was something else. Something disturbing. For whenever her mother mentioned the boy, the face that flashed into Jenna's mind was no longer some imagined face. It wasn't the face of some monstrous criminal. Nothing like that. And, surprisingly, it wasn't Joe Sadowski's face, either. Because the face she kept seeing, over and over, no matter how hard she tried to block it from her mind, was the familiar face of Michael MacKenzie.

the healing

25

In the early-morning hours on the day before Labor Day, Jenna dreams of the Ghost Tree and of her father. Her father never speaks in the dream. But he does take her by the hand. In that moment everything around them disappears except for the night sky, so thick with stars that Jenna feels she is inhaling them with every breath she takes. And it must be true, because her skin has become transparent with light. She is not seeing with her eyes. She knows this because she is able to take in everything above and below. All without moving an inch.

She sees that the billions of stars surrounding her aren't floating all alone in dark space, as she has always imagined. Not at all. Now she sees how fine shimmering threads, like the filaments of a delicate spiderweb glistening with dew, weave the stars together in one splendid design. And when she looks at her father, she sees that the silvery threads also connect the two of them, and she knows these are threads that can never be broken.

When she awakens, Jenna rises, and, although it is still a few hours before dawn, she dresses, tiptoes downstairs, and leaves by the back door. She goes to the garage to find her bike. It has been a while since she last rode it, and it wobbles beneath her for the first few blocks. Her house is on a hill. She has forgotten how difficult it is to pedal up the steep incline and now grunts and groans her way upward. She is pedaling for dear life; she is pedaling her way to the Great Swamp.

Overhead, the stars look as they always have. But Jenna isn't fooled. Because even though her eyes tell her otherwise, she knows now that some things can be seen only with the heart.

michael is also awake. He has been awake most of the night. He knows what he must do, but it terrifies him. Still, he cannot go on as he has these past two months. The deception must end. And only he can end it.

He understands now that he has been carrying the stone in his throat all this time. He hasn't swallowed it at all, and he is drowning.

At the pool, earlier in the day, he thought about what he would say to the police. He thought about going to the station right from work, but he went home instead. He is a coward, and he hates himself for it.

He lies awake for hours, his sheets growing damp with his fear. When he finally falls asleep, he dreams of Charlie Ward.

He does not remember much of the dream, only the face of Charlie Ward. He knows it's Charlie Ward because he recognizes him from his picture in the newspapers. In the dream, Charlie Ward slaps him on the back as if they're old friends, then puts his arm around Michael's shoulder. Michael isn't the least bit afraid, though he thinks he ought to be. He doesn't remember the rest of the dream, but when he wakes up, he realizes that for the first time in weeks he can breathe without feeling a great weight pressing on his chest.

He sits on the edge of the bed, watching the full moon outside his window, and in those moments he knows what he must do. While it is still dark, while the cicadas buzz-saw their background music, Michael dresses and heads straight for the garage to find the shovel.

He digs nonstop for almost an hour. The logs from the woodpile lie in a random heap beside the large hole. And even though he is wearing only a thin T-shirt, sweat coats his face and runs along his sides, soaking the soft cotton. The cool night air ripples in chilling waves across his skin whenever he stops to take a breath. But although his arms ache, he keeps at it until the clunk of the shovel tells him he has finally hit the PVC pipe that hides the Winchester.

He does not bother to fill in the hole or restack the wood. It's not important. He will tell them where he hid the gun during those long weeks, and they will come to this spot and see for themselves. He doesn't even bother to wipe the dirt from his hands or from the PVC pipe. But he does unseal the end caps and remove the rifle. And when he holds the gun in his hands for the first time since the night he buried it, he expects to feel the same wave of nausea he felt the last time he held it. But it doesn't come. Instead he feels a strong sense of purpose. He knows this isn't just about keeping Joe out of more trouble. This is about him. About Michael MacKenzie. And about who he is.

Then, without turning on the ignition, he pushes his father's Honda to the end of the driveway and onto the street. Carefully he sets the rifle beside him on the passenger seat and starts the car. He and the Winchester are partners in crime. They will make this journey together.

Jenna rides her bike along the trail through the dark forest of the Great Swamp while the cool night air numbs her earlobes, and never once does she think of tangled vines grabbing her.

She understands what the dream has been trying to tell her, and she knows why she is making this journey. She needs to put things to rest. She also knows her way of doing this might not seem like reasonable behavior to some. But she doesn't care. She has begun to think that maybe the mind has different ways of knowing.

She knows now that it was Michael MacKenzie who fired the shot that killed her father. She knows this in a way that she isn't used to knowing. But she trusts her instincts. The knowledge doesn't weigh nearly as heavily on her as she had thought it would. She doesn't hate him, as she had expected to. She no longer wants to make him pay for what he's done. She understands, intuitively, that he has been trying to tell her all along. And she has already decided that the next time she sees him sitting on the church steps, she will walk right up to him and give him his chance.

When Jenna finally comes to the Ghost Tree, she sees how the moon, full and ripe, lights the space around the tree more brightly than any streetlight, so that she will not stumble in the dark. Then she leaves her bike by the side of the trail, climbs into the cradle of the ancient sycamore, and waits.

In spite of the cool air, she feels the same warmth and comfort, sitting in the old tree, that she knew on that frosty winter afternoon when her father brought her here to feed the deer. She leans back against one of the upper trunks and gazes up through the branches. If the legend is true, her ancestors are there beside her, and so is her father. It doesn't matter that she can't see them; she welcomes them anyway.

She understands that her mind has been trying to show her a way in which to begin to heal herself. That is what the dreams have been about. They have reminded her of a place that she shared with her father. A place that held a special meaning.

On this night she will see her father again. She will tell him how much she misses him, how she wishes she could have saved him from what happened. She needs to tell him these things. She needs to let go.

And perhaps the ancient ones will dance around her, chanting their wisdom. But most of all, she wants to believe, as she huddles closer to the tree, that this place, as her father once told her, is a place of healing.

michael drives down Main Street. Fluorescent lights spill their cold white glow through the store windows onto the sidewalks outside. He can't take his eyes off the metal gates that protect the storefronts. They remind him of steel prison bars, and his body shudders involuntarily.

He turns up Jenna Ward's street. His plan is to wait on the church steps until morning, and then he will knock on her front door. He wants to talk to her first, before he goes to the police. Because once he turns himself in, he knows he might not have a chance to see her alone.

He will also tell the police about Joe. He will say he swore his friend to secrecy. He will tell them Joe did what he did out of loyalty, because this is true. And maybe that will count for something.

Michael pulls the car up in front of the church. There is at least another hour until dawn. He wonders what will happen if the Hangman drives by again and sees him sitting on the steps at this hour. He will probably ask him to move on, or charge him with vagrancy. Maybe he will want to search the car. Michael looks over at the Winchester, trying to decide what to do.

Then he stares across the street at Jenna's house. Even though it's still night, the moonlight reflects off the second-story windows, making it seem as if there is a light on inside.

There is no place else to go at this hour. Not even Amy's house. And he is beginning to grow nervous at the thought of what the morning holds. He decides it is better just to drive around for a while. It will keep his mind occupied. The last thing he wants to do is back out. He has to get through this somehow. That's when he remembers the Ghost Tree.

When he gets to the Great Swamp, Michael parks the car in the lot by the information center. Then he takes the rifle and follows the trail that leads to the Ghost Tree. He knows why he has come. He is testing his courage.

The moonlight, brighter than he can ever remember, lights his way along the path, as dark shadows leak from tree stumps like oil spills. In the background he hears the owls calling to each other. Their mournful hoots echo as far as the sound will carry. Michael is reminded of sounds flowing through telephone lines. This is how the owls stay connected, he thinks. This is how they remind each other they are not alone in the forest.

As he rounds the last bend he can just make out the tree up ahead. And when he is only a few yards away, he is stunned to find Jenna Ward curled into its cradle, sleeping soundly.

Nothing in his experience has prepared him for this. Because such things simply do not happen.

But as he stands there, pressing the rifle to his chest, he wonders if, just maybe, he is supposed to be here, that he has been coming here to meet Jenna Ward all along.

He wonders if, like him, she has come to confront her own personal ghosts. And as he watches her sleeping so peacefully, with just the slightest hint of a smile at the corners of her mouth, it is hard for him to imagine the pain she must have endured these long weeks. Yet he does not try to fool himself; he knows she has suffered. Still, he clings to that trace of a smile on Jenna's lips, because he knows that their meeting, when she awakens, will be the hardest thing he has ever done in his life. This is what swallowing stones is all about.

Michael lets the soft, mellow hooting of the owls wash over him as he sits down on a large boulder a few yards from the tree. He waits. The rifle lies across his knees like the gift he intends it to be; then, worried that it might alarm Jenna, he lays the gun on the ground behind the rock. For this is the only thing he has left to give: the truth. And Jenna Ward will be the first one to hear it. Then he will take the rifle and his story to Ralph Healey.

Michael is glad that it is almost dawn. He wants them to meet in daylight, so that Jenna can see his face. He owes her that. And as he waits, he begins to think that maybe coming to this place isn't about old legends or proving how brave you are. Maybe it is about facing the things that haunt you.

So as the early-morning sunlight sends its first rays across the horizon, Michael keeps watch over Jenna, just as he did on those other evening vigils when he sat across from her house on the church steps. Only this time, when she awakens, he will be there waiting.